PRAISE FOR ASA MARIA BRADLEY'S WORK

"When it comes to paranormal romance with explosive action scenes, Bradley has that nailed…. *Loki Ascending* is a riveting adventure tale with a thrilling climax to match."
~*Entertainment Weekly*

"Action-packed, sexy, and fun! Reminiscent of J.R. Ward—but with Vikings!"
~Ilona Andrews, *New York Times* Bestselling Author for *Viking Warrior Rebel*

"An entertaining read when you like crime stories with a touch of paranormal and shape-shifting."
~Honest Bookworm for *Flash of Fear*

"…a swoon-worthy hero who sizzles across the pages in this tale full of passion, blood, and destiny! Sexy, stubborn, and smart lovers clash in a tension-filled race to outwit science and control fate."
~Rebecca Zanetti, *New York Times* Bestselling Author for *Viking Warrior Rising*

"Bradley's story is a whirlwind of action, suspense, humor, and a ton of romance! …you'll be reading this page-turner the whole day!"

~*Bookstr* for *Loki Ascending*

"Nonstop action, satisfying romantic encounters, and intriguing world building make this a thoroughly enjoyable paranormal-romance series."

~*Booklist* for *Viking Warrior Rising*

"...blends Norse mythology and evil government experiments into an unusual paranormal...the immortal Viking premise is perfect for paranormal romance readers who are looking for something different."

~*Publishers Weekly* for *Viking Warrior Rising*

A WOLF'S HUNGER

ASA MARIA BRADLEY

KAERING LLC

For Ellen and Eric. You impress me every day.
I am so proud and honored to be your aunt!

CHAPTER 1

*L*eaning back against the bar of Dev Beat, a popular San Francisco nightclub, Laney Marconi tugged on the hem of her short black dress and took a sip of her club soda. She'd asked the bartender to garnish the glass with a slice of lime so that it looked like a gin and tonic. The drink and the outfit were all part of her disguise to look like a regular club patron. Blue and purple ceiling strobe lights pulsed in time with the loud music screaming from the speakers. The oval-shaped bar's lighting display was made entirely of cobalt neon lights strategically placed to make the counter and the liquor shelves in the middle look as if carved out of ice. A suitable environment in which to hunt a Swedish wolf.

Laney smiled to herself, but when one of the men at the bar took that as an invitation to take a step closer, she quickly schooled her features into her regular resting-bitch-face. A snooty head-toss flipped the long red tresses of her wig over her shoulder as she dismissed the guy and continued on her circumvent path around the bar, closer and closer to her target this evening, Arek Varg.

Since he wasn't looking her way, Laney took a moment to study him through a mirror on the wall opposite. She'd never met him but knew of him through his reputation. Or maybe lack of reputation was a better expression because security around the head alpha of the western wolf packs was locked down tight. Laney had scoured the internet for information, but Mr. Varg had no social media presence.

His company's website provided only information about their security services, nothing about its handsome owner. Arek Varg's short blond hair and azure blue eyes betrayed his Scandinavian origin, and the tailored cornflower-colored button-down shirt he wore deepened his eyes' color. He looked like he should be in a movie or on a billboard.

She kept watching Varg through the wall of mirrors as she positioned herself on the opposite side from where he sat at the race-track shaped bar. Even though the bar staff flittered between them as they filled drink orders, and that glass shelf system filled with bottles of alcohol occupied the middle, she could still see him. He kept looking at his phone. Maybe to check the time, or perhaps to check for incoming messages.

Laney's client had assured her they'd make sure Varg came to the bar at this precise time. She had no idea what they'd use to lure him there. Her job was just to recover the stolen artifact that Varg wore around his neck. She was too far away to see the medallion, but the pictures had shown a platinum wolf head inscribed with runes and three interlocking triangles. At first, she'd been surprised to receive the files that showed the wealthy shifter was her new target. Although not many details about Varg's personal life or background were public, he was known within the supernatural community as being upstanding and honest, if a bit archaic in some of his leadership theories. The only few rumblings she'd been able to dig up about the popular alpha were about members who had stepped out of bounds of the pack rules being punished a little too severely by Varg's enforcer.

But none of that was Laney's concern. The only thing she needed to worry about was to recover the stolen talisman for the insurance company that had hired her. She may have fallen far from her former prestigious academic position, but she still prided herself on doing her job quickly and professionally. Besides, the heels she'd chosen to wear with the black dress were pinching her toes, and she wanted to get home and exchange her party outfit for comfy slippers and pajamas. She slowly strode along the bar as if she was looking for an opening among the throng gathered at the counter so she could order another drink from the bartender.

She needed to be close enough to be ready to strike when the perfect opportunity presented itself, but not so near that she attracted Varg's attention or, goddess forbid, made eye contact. She'd learned the hard way that people better remembered individuals they'd looked in the eye, even if only for a fleeting moment.

Five people separated them now.

Laney sipped her drink as she once again used the mirrors to keep an eye on her mark. She tapped her toe impatiently and squelched the butterflies in her stomach. It was always like this right before the action started, nerves mixed with excitement and anticipation. Later on, once she was back home and safe in her apartment, the adrenaline crash would make her exhausted, but right now, that same adrenaline sharpened her senses and provided her with hyperfocus.

She knew it was all in her imagination, but it was as if despite the loud music, she could hear the rustling of Varg's shirt's expensive fabric caressing the skin of his arm as he

3

turned the phone to look at the time again. The impatient sight that left his lips caressed her ears. She even felt the warmth from his body as irritation heated his blood.

Finally, what she'd been waiting for happened.

A tall brunette in a slinky red dress that perfectly draped and displayed her curves approached Varg. The woman placed her elbow on the bar and leaned to face Varg, her back toward Laney, who quickly decreased the distance between herself and the target until she was right behind the woman, but facing the bar. Frankly, Laney was surprised that it had taken this long for anyone to try to flirt with Varg. Maybe it was his grim expression and impatient energy that kept potential hookups away. What was the male equivalent of resting bitch face? Resting jerk face? Resting dick face?

She smiled to herself again, and the bartender stopped as she passed by. "Can I get you another one?" the petite woman with bright purple hair gestured toward Laney's drink.

"Oh no, I'm fine," she answered, and the bartender continued toward one of the many other patrons gesturing for refills.

Crap, she'd gotten caught up in her own musings and the bartender's question. Rule number one, never take your eyes off the target. She angled her body so she could catch a glimpse of what Varg and the woman conversing.

The temptress in the red dress had good game. She'd cocked a hip against the bar and flicked her hair over one shoulder. A sultry smile played on her lips, and she'd slightly lowered her eyelids as she traced a finger on the rim of her glass of red wine.

Laney almost felt sorry for Varg or whoever did his laundry, but hopefully, the stain would come out of that beautiful shirt he was wearing. She twisted so that she bumped into the brunette. As the other woman splashed the handsome wolf alpha with wine, Laney slipped around her, heading straight toward Varg.

A quick burst of power channeled through her fingertips broke the medallion's chain around the alpha's neck, and Laney kept moving as she slipped the artifact down her cleavage. She joined the crowd on the dance floor. Raising her arms above her head, she closed her eyes and abandoned her body to the rhythm of the music. Her hips swayed as she danced herself closer to the middle of the floor so that more and more people shielded her from the soaked alpha. The medallion heated her skin as it lay nestled in nestled between her breasts, and she resisted the temptation to tap into its magic and find out how many centuries old it was. She needed to transport it to a parallel dimension quickly, in case she got caught.

When she'd been Dr. Marconi in the Anthropology and Archeology department at the university, she'd used her powers over earthbound materials only to evaluate and date historical artifacts. She'd never shared her shifting dimensions ability because making items disappear would be considered by her colleagues as either a cheap party trick or something suspicious because it could be used to steal priceless objects.

Now that skill was her primary source of income. She refused to give in to the feeling of shame that sometimes came over her when she thought about how low she'd sunk.

Tomorrow, she'd meet with the insurance company representatives, who would then return the artifact to its rightful owner. Like many of their competitors, they'd rather hire an independent contractor to recover the items instead of calling the police. That way, they could keep news about items stolen out of the press. Returning objects to their rightful owner gave Laney a small sense of pride, but mostly she cared about the check they'd give her that would finally make it possible to pay her outstanding bills and rent.

She brought her arms down again and covered her chest with her palms as she kept dancing. She guided her power into the medallion, deeper and deeper until the platinum metal vibrated on a molecular level. A half-second later, she felt it disappearing beyond the space she and the other dancers occupied. Its presence was still with her, but it was a different her, another Laney. That woman danced in a club just like this one, with the artifact still nestled in her cleavage, but to Laney, she appeared hazy, as if in a dream.

All she had to do now was maintain the connection with that other Laney until she got back to her apartment. Once there, she'd ask for the medallion back and then lock it away in the safe in her apartment.

CHAPTER 2

*A*rek paced his office, glaring at his two closest friends, who also happened to be his second-in-command wolves. "How the hell could this happen?" he addressed to the room at large. He wished he'd chosen solid heavy wood for his desk and bookcases instead of the modern chrome and glass. He felt like hitting something, but the furniture would shatter, and he didn't feel like dealing with the mess of slivers.

Bolt, who lazily reclined in one of the black leather visitors chairs in front of Arek's desk, chose to answer. "You went out without us, again." His voice sounded calm, but his ordinarily hazel eyes were now bottle green—a sign of Bolt's alert and unhappy wolf. The unhappy part, Arek felt even though he wasn't wearing his Odin medallion. His lieutenants were part of his own pack, and as their alpha, he connected with them easily. But as the Commanding Alpha of the Western packs, he needed to tap into every pack and required the Odin medallion as his focus. A detail he hadn't shared with anyone—including the men in this office—but rumors about the talisman's magical properties had flown wild for ages. The latest outrageous story he'd heard involved him teleporting.

The medallion didn't hold true magic. However, as a symbol of Arek and his wolves serving Odin and Freya as Ulfheidnar—elite soldiers who could take the shape of wolves—it worked as a focus for pack magic. As far as he knew, none of the other alphas in the Western Packs Coalition, or any other coalition, had anything like it.

Justice occupied the other chair, and his crisp British voice drawled out, "Fuck mate, our duty is to keep you safe and carry out your orders, but you make the job ridiculously hard with your need to be the lone wolf." His eyes momentarily flashed purple, but then Justice blinked, and they returned to his human grayish silver. The man kept all his emotions bottled up and had a reputation for being stone cold in all situations. It served him well as the coalition packs' enforcer.

Arek adjusted the collar of his shirt. Red wine still stained the garment, but at least it had dried now. "What the fuck was I supposed to do. You were both out, and the caller insisted we meet immediately. "He knew that sounded ridiculous as soon as he said the words, but he felt this childish need to defend himself. Worst of all, he knew Justice was right.

Bolt studied him with those eerie green eyes, his voice still even as ever. "And you didn't think there was something off about the fact that the caller chose a night club as a meeting point? A place full of people, despite that he insisted on keeping his identity hidden and seemed to be on the run from someone?"

"The information was important." Arek defended himself again. "Too important to worry about the details of the meeting place."

Justice raised a dark eyebrow but remained quiet.

"Okay fine, I should have waited for one of you to get back," Arek threw out.

"Or at least taken one of the other wolves with you," Bolt interjected.

"Yes," Arek conceded through clenched teeth. He knew both of them were correct, but he'd wanted to go on his own to check out if the information was useful. He'd foolishly thought he could keep the meeting from Bolt if it weren't. Fuck, he was an idiot. He should have known it was a trap. And now the Odin medallion was gone. Anger flowed through his body and sharpened his senses. The wolf inside him awoke and almost purred. The beast loved anger.

"What was this vital information?" Justice asked, his eyes glimmered purple again in response to Arek's wolf coming out.

Despite the top button being open, Arek's shirt felt constricted. He snapped the second open as well. It didn't help. "He said he knew where Arrow is." Arek avoided looking at Bolt, but out of the corner of his eye, he could see the man snapping to attention.

"What the fuck?" Bolt growled. Any mention of his twin brother pissed him off, but Arek could also sense longing and sorrow behind that anger. Not that he'd ever let Bolt know. The two brothers were estranged, but Bolt wouldn't reveal the details. "You put yourself in danger because of Arrow, and you didn't include me?"

Justice held out a hand to calm the other man. "What about Arrow?"

Arek pinched the bridge of his nose. "I never found out. The caller said he knew where Arrow might be." He finally met Bolt's gaze. "I thought I'd check it out for you, to see if it was legit." He shrugged apologetically. He'd tried to protect his lieutenant from any false hope. But Arrow had been pack, family, and therefore still one of Arek's wolves. Once pack, always pack, until he formally rescinded Arek as his alpha.

Justice chimed in. "We'll figure out who set this up, mate. But right now, let's concentrate on the actual thief."

Arek nodded. "We don't have to reveal the artifact's true importance. People know the necklace belonged to my grandfather. And in addition to it having sentimental value, as Commanding Alpha, I can't let anyone get away with stealing from me. I would lose respect." The medallion's role in his ability to emotionally connect with packs other than his own could be construed as witchcraft. Wolves were suspicious of any true magic since it could manipulate them if they didn't tap into pack magic quickly enough. Arek didn't share the prejudice against all magic but had collected as many magical artifacts as he could during the years he'd been a wolf. That way, they couldn't hurt his or any other shifters. "It's been less than an hour since the thief got the medallion. We should be able to catch them, or at least identify them before morning."

Bolt growled again but then relaxed in his seat.

"I'm already on it," Justice said, holding up a tablet. "The club sent over the security videos from the cameras covering the bar. I've isolated the one that had the best angle to overview Arek's spot in the bar." He reached for the remote control that turned on the fifty-inch flatscreen on the wall and clicked the power button. A few taps on the tablet made the video feed display on the larger screen.

Arek watched the black and white images of himself sitting in the bar, impatiently tapping his fingers and checking his phone. "Fast forward," he said, and Justice did as asked but then slowed the feed to regular speed as a brown-haired woman in the red dress approached Arek on the screen.

"It took a while before any of the females approached you," Bolt said. "You may be losing your touch."

Arek didn't bother to answer but allowed his wolf a short growl, which caused Justice to chuckle.

When Bolt joined in, Arek's shirt finally didn't feel so tight anymore. According to Norse mythology, Odin always had two loyal wolves at his side, Geri and Freki. Not that he compared himself to the All Father, but Arek often felt like Bolt and Justice were his true loyal companions.

Two loyal companions who didn't mind giving him shit. They weren't wrong, though. Usually, Arek had plenty of female attention, but he didn't blame the women in the bar for not talking to him. Even on the screen, he could see a cloud of irritation and anger surrounding him. His face was pinched and brow furrowed. He felt sorry for the poor woman who had been brave enough to approach him. Not only had she gotten an earful when she spilled her wine on him by accident, but she'd then had to put up with being interrogated after the medallion had disappeared. He'd been so busy wiping his shirt that he hadn't associated the slight sting on his neck with someone breaking the chain and stealing the jewelry right off his neck.

It hadn't taken long to figure out that the brunette wasn't in on the theft. She'd just been in the wrong place at the wrong time. Arek had apologized, but her face when she left showed how much she regretted hitting on him that night. It was a shame because she was quite attractive. Normally he'd been very receptive to her flirtations, but the promised news of Arrow had distracted him.

The version of himself on the video was busy wiping off his shirt when something on the screen caught real-time Arek's eye. "Stop," he barked out. "Back it up a few frames."

Justice paused the footage, and the three of them leaned

closer toward the flatscreen on the wall. "What do you see," Bolt asked.

"That woman behind the brunette," Arek said. "The one who's talking with the bartender. Her drink is almost empty, but she's not ordering another one."

"Maybe she'd had enough," Bolt suggested.

The hairs on the back of Arek's neck stood. "No, there's something off about how she's holding herself. She's talking to the bartender, who's standing slightly to the right of her. And yet, the woman's face is angled to the left."

Bolt stood and walked closer to the flatscreen. "She's looking at you."

"I'm slowing down the video," Justice said, and the footage moved in slow motion as they watched the woman on the screen.

Arek studied her slim athletic build. Racking his brain to see if she looked like anyone he knew. If it were anyone who'd shared his bed, he would know her body in detail. He may not offer any of his lovers' commitment, but he always took his time learning their bodies so he could find out how to please them properly.

The woman had her back toward the camera, and her face was in profile, so there wasn't much he could see. She had long, red hair and wore a short black dress that was revealing enough to show off some curves but not tight enough to garner too much attention. She'd dressed like someone who would fit in perfectly on the club scene but not stand out—the perfect outfit for a small jewelry heist.

As they watched, the woman put her drink on the bar and slipped out of frame right at the moment when the brunette spilled her drink on Arek. "Where did she go," he asked.

"I'm looking for her." Justice tapped furiously on the tablet. "Got her."

The flatscreen flickered, and a new viewpoint of the bar

displayed—this one from further away and higher. Part of the dance floor behind where Arek had been sitting was now visible. Arek watched the repeated conversation between the mystery woman in the black dress and the bartender. This time when the woman slipped away, they could see her in the frame. If Justice hadn't slowed down the footage's speed, Arek would have missed the woman's elbow's slight nudge into the back of the brunette in the red dress.

"Fuck, she pushed her," Justice said.

It looked like the mystery woman in the video briefly touched Arek's shoulder as she slipped by him. But he knew that was the moment the medallion had disappeared. That must have been the exact moment he'd felt the sting on his neck. He rubbed the spot where his skin had been zapped. "She's the one who took the Odin medallion." His tone took on the darkness of the anger coursing through his veins.

Justice rewound the footage. "Are you sure? I didn't see her steal it."

"Certain," Arek answered. "Find out who she is."

"Do you know her?" Bolt asked.

"I do not," Arek answered, now sure he'd never met the woman before. "But we will get to know each other soon." A grim smile stretched his lips as he turned to face his two lieutenants. "Hunt her down and bring her to me."

CHAPTER 3

*L*aney checked the address on the business card she'd received from Mr. Hartford the last time she'd visited the Global Securities offices. Just like the other five times she'd looked at the little piece of stiff paper, the address was the same as when she'd met with Mr. Hartford at this location five days ago. The difference being though that on that occasion, the lobby had a receptionist working hard to answer the phones that were ringing off the hook, the hallways had been filled with busy employees walking and talking while carrying folders, and the glass-walled offices had been equipped with not just furniture and computers, but actual people had been using said computers to work supposedly.

In short, it had been very different from the desolate, empty office landscape that greeted her now. There were no people, no furniture, and definitely no phones or computers. The only things indicating that this had been a busy place of business once were the indentations that the desks and chairs had left in the carpet.

Laney's stomach churned, and nausea rose in the back of her throat. This was not a good sign.

She'd walked into the building just like last time, not really noticing, but now thinking twice about that the security guard on the entrance floor had been absent. She'd taken the elevator to the tenth floor of the building, just like she did her previous visit. What in the world had happened since then? Did the company go bankrupt?

She pulled out her phone and called the number on Mr. Hartford's business card, almost expecting a phantom phone start to ring from one of the offices. She'd already checked them all, though, and they were all very empty. Signal after signal echoed down the phone line as she waited for someone to pick up. Nobody did.

After a while, her phone disconnected the call automatically.

Refusing to acknowledge what was slowly becoming painfully clear, she stubbornly hit redial—same result.

Her knees gave out, and she sunk to the floor. This was bad on so many levels. Tears welled in her eyes. If this insurance company was fake, the mission had been fake, which meant she'd just stolen a magical artifact from the Commanding Alpha of the western packs.

Laney rubbed her forehead and willed her tears to stop.

Think. Think hard.

How to return the medallion to Varg before he found her?

Maybe she could turn the medallion into the police and say she'd found it.

She dismissed the idea, shuddering as she remembered how much havoc a magical item could wreak if in regular human hands, or even worse, a human who had just a little bit of power but didn't know how to use it.

A few decades back, a human-led archaeological dig in Italy had discovered a powerful ancient Christian relic. The baptismal font had looked like any other old stone basin but had, in fact, harnessed magic.

The archaeologists had placed the find in a monastery church not far from the dig site. Unfortunately, one of the nuns of the order who worshipped in the church had, during prayer, uttered the exact piece of Latin scripture necessary to awaken the magic within the font.

It had filled with water and kept on filling until it overflowed the church, the monastery, the village, and the surrounding countryside. Witches and mages from several universities had to combine their powers to stop the water. The mainstream media had reported the incident as a freak flash flood. But among magic practitioners, it became a case study for why gifted humans shouldn't meddle with magic.

Now, university departments, such as the one that Laney had belonged to, kept track of all archeological findings, just in case they were infused with power.

But thinking about her past life as the darling of the witches and mages' academic world always hurt, so Laney quickly turned her mind away from that. "I guess I could construct some sort of box to return the item. One that dampens the powers or shields it?" She wondered out loud.

"That's a great idea. Unfortunately, you will not have the chance to put it in practice," a voice accented heavily with Russian said.

Laney's head snapped up, and she jumped to her feet, stumbling backward.

A man entirely dressed in black stood before her. How had she not heard anyone approaching? Then the stench of dark magic reached her nose, and she knew he must have cloaked himself.

"Who are you?" Her voice held steady, but her insides shook. Dark magic required a blood sacrifice, and the heavy smell emitting from the man indicated he'd done several.

Chills raced up her spine. She thought she'd been in trouble before, with a pissed off alpha wolf looking for her. If dark magic practitioners were involved, she was infinitely more screwed.

He smiled, but it didn't reach his eyes. They were so dark that Laney couldn't tell where his pupil ended and the iris started. "One of your old acquaintances, in need of help." His face was a mismatch of blurry features.

She'd never be able to describe him to anyone. The magic cloaking was as effective as if he'd worn a mask but much more menacing. He seemed the type who liked menacing, even if it required more energy than just pulling on a piece of cloth.

And she could see why. Not being able to focus on the face of the person she spoke with freaked out Laney's senses, increasing her nausea. The only thing she could tell for sure was that someone broke his nose at some point. No matter which shapes the face shifted between, it remained crocked.

She took a step back. "I have never met you before, and I don't see how I will be able to help you." Brave words for a terrified woman, but she refused to show her fear.

"You already have." The man took a step closer. He moved with the fluid grace of a shifter, but he didn't give off a shifter vibe. Maybe he cloaked that too.

Laney scrambled further back. "Get away from me." So much for not showing how scared she was.

The man's outline shimmered, and all of a sudden, Mr. Hartford stood in front of her.

She gasped and tried to swallow the sound while at the same time push down the big lump of dread lodged in her throat. The result came out as an undignified gulp.

His kind brown eyes twinkled as he looked at her. "I'm hurt you don't recognize me, Dr. Marconi. I so enjoyed our previous conversation," Mr. Hartford said in his generic

American accent. His body shimmered again, and his voice changed into the one with a Russian accent. The black-clad man stood in front of her again. "And I will definitely enjoy our future...conversations." The pause made Laney's stomach clench. She had a strong feeling that what he referred to as conversation would be more like an inter-rogation.

Probably an "enhanced" interrogation. Laney swallowed hard.

Considering he chose just to disguise his face, which consumed less magic than a full transformation, he was probably conserving his energy for their "conversation."

Her own magic was strong but limited to earth materials. Everything in this office was synthetic. She frantically looked around, trying to spot something made of metal or stone. Technically she should be able to manipulate glass since it originated from sand, soda ash, and sandstone. Still, as a human-made compound, it required more energy to bend to her will than she'd ever been able to harness.

Besides, against dark magic, she was pretty much helpless.

But she refused to give up.

Maybe if she kept him talking, some sort of solution would present itself. *Yeah, right*, the sarcastic voice inside her head whispered, but she squelched it. "What do you want?" She took another step and bumped into the wall behind her. "And how did you cloak your magic from me when we met last time?"

The man didn't bother getting closer. "I don't share my trade secrets." He smiled again, with just as little warmth as previously. "And I want the medallion, of course. After all, we paid you a lot of money to retrieve it for us."

Laney wondered briefly who "we" referred to but dismissed the thought and concentrated on how to get out of this impossible situation. "You hired me under false pretenses, though." Internally, she debated on how wise it was to contradict him, but anything to keep *this* conversation going, so she didn't have to think about the future ones that the man had promised.

"I gave you all the paperwork that you requested." He tilted his head. "And you seemed very satisfied with them."

It was true. The paperwork that "Mr. Hartford" had presented had all checked out. He'd given Laney an authentication certificate and several documents that proved ownership. Obviously, they'd all been fakes. Excellent fakes because she had double and triple checked their authenticity like she always did, and those documents had all been on record at various government agencies.

"But you knew they were fake," Laney insisted, her voice squeaking a little at the end of the sentence. She cleared her throat. "So, you violated the ethics clause I put in my contract."

The man threw his head back and laughed loudly. The shifting of his facial features sped up, and Laney had to swallow hard to keep from throwing up.

The faint sound of sirens wafted up to the floor on which they were. A small flicker of hope rose in Laney's chest even though she knew the first responders had nothing to do with her.

The man's laughter ended as abruptly as it had begun. "Enough," he said, throwing out his arm.

A bolt of magic hit Laney square in the chest. She struggled to inhale, and then everything went dark.

CHAPTER 4

*A*rek looked around the unassuming apartment in the Bernal Heights neighborhood of San Francisco. Either Dr. Elaine Marconi's housekeeping skills were sorely lacking, or her home had been ransacked. He'd bet on the latter.

He stood by a dining room table that had been cleaved in two. What he assumed were the matching chairs now looked mostly fit to be kindling.

Considering that the building had a doorman and outside security cameras, this didn't seem a likely place for a random robbery. Plus, whoever broke in had taken the time to pick the lock and close the door after themselves. Intruders that didn't want to be noticed but yet had demolished the interior.

The entire apartment, except for the bedroom, had an open plan layout. You could stand anywhere and see everything else. Arek walked into the kitchen area, where the marble counter lay crushed into several pieces. Whoever had broken it had beyond-human strength. Based on the deep gashes marring the stone, he'd bet shifters of some kind.

Every cupboard had been opened, and the content shoved out. Arek tried to avoid stepping on the mess of broken dishes, glasses, and spilled food on the floor, but it was impossible. Finally, he gave up and crunched his way out of the kitchen and over to where a shredded couch sat in front of a shattered big flat screen.

Bolt stood in front of where the screen had hung on the wall. "That's a Q900R screen," sadness tinted his voice. "It's top of the line and retails for almost forty K." He flicked one of the wires poking out of a hole in the wall. "I get opening all the cabinets. But what did they think she was hiding inside her TV?"

Arek nodded. "This was more than searching for something. I assume the medallion. This is someone taking out their rage. She must have pissed them off."

"Maybe she held out for more money before she gave them the necklace." Bolt sniffed the air. "There was more than one person here. And they reek of magic."

Arek drew in a deep breath. Bolt was right, the stink of magic lingered in the air, but it was worse than that. "Not just any magic. Dark magic."

"Fuck," Bolt breathed out, looking around as if someone would jump out at them.

"Did you find anything about this woman performing blood sacrifices?"

His lieutenant shook his head. "No. I had to dig pretty deep into her file to determine why she'd left the university. I'd found out if she were a dark witch." Bolt had spent most of the morning running facial recognition software on various databases until he'd found their medallion thief in a university employment record. After that, it was easy to figure out where she lived. Dr. Elaine Marconi had once been a revered expert on magical artifacts but fell from grace when she slept with one of her students. Now she made her living as a thief for hire.

Arek looked around the apartment again. The place wasn't high-end, but not cheap either. San Francisco rents ran higher than average since water surrounded the city on three sides. There was no more land to build on unless you went south, down the peninsula. The interior of the place spoke, though, of an expensive taste. Even-though everything was in tatters, Arek could see it was all excellent quality. He almost felt sorry for Dr. Marconi having to replace all the furniture. Even the comfortable plush couch had become a target for the shifters' anger. White fluffs of stuffing spilled out of deep gashes in the cushions. "Everything is smashed to pieces, but I don't see or smell any blood. Do you think she was here, and they took her?"

Bolt shook his head, still staring at the torn wires sticking out of the wall. "No. And if they came to grab her, why stick around and demolish the place?"

Arek left Bolt to contemplate the sad fate of the TV and walked into the woman's bedroom. Shreds of fabric covered the floor. He couldn't tell if it was bedding or curtains.

The mattress leaned against a wall. Its springs wholly exposed. Fine fragments of wood that could at one point have been her box spring covered the floor.

A big hole in the wall had the same size as the collapsed dresser that lay beneath it. The drawers had pieces of bright colored silky cloth spilled from the destroyed drawers. He hunched down and poked at one of them with a fingertip. Dr. Marconi's expensive taste included fine underwear.

Once again, he sniffed the air, trying to get a reading on who had destroyed the place, but the dark magic made it impossible to lock down on a scent trail. Still no smell of blood, though.

He returned to Bolt, who had rigged up his laptop and

rapidly typed on the keyboard while staring at the screen, a deep furrow on his brow.

Arek looked around again. "Why all this anger?" he wondered out loud. "I don't think they found what they were looking for."

"I agree," Bolt said, turning the computer so that the screen faced Arek. "There were two wolves here, but they somehow cloaked themselves when they were in the elevator and hallway. The only security footage I could get is when they were in here and didn't bother hiding."

Arek glanced around the apartment, first now noticing small cameras in the corners of the room. "Fuck, I didn't think about us getting caught on video inside her apartment."

"I did," Bolt said. "I disabled the cameras everywhere in the building before we went in." They'd snuck up through the parking garage to bypass the doorman. Arek knew Bolt had disabled the cameras in the garage, but apparently, his lieutenant had thought further than that.

He leaned in to see what Bolt had uncovered by hacking into the surveillance system. Two men searched through the apartment. At first, they went methodically from room to room, opening and closing drawers and cabinets. The only thing giving them away as not being human was their constant scenting of the air. Arek guessed he and Bolt would look like that on the footage, too, if it weren't for the forethought of his lieutenant.

Dr. Marconi seemed to have used her dining room table as a home office. She'd pushed up against the wall and placed a lone chair beside it. The other chairs had been stacked in a corner. A laptop and piles of papers covered it. One of the wolves shifted partially, and his hands sprung large claws that he used to shred the documents and destroy the laptop.

"Stupid," Bolt muttered. "There could be useful information on that computer."

"Do you know who they are?" Arek asked. His lieutenant had a photographic memory when it came to faces and pelt patterns. The wolves on the screen grew impatient. Instead of methodically searching through shelves and drawers, they now shoved everything out and flung it around.

"Nope. Unless someone has recruits, we don't know about. They're not part of any of the Western Packs."

"They should have reported new pack members," Arek said slowly. Did he have a mutiny on his hands? Could one of the alphas that reported to him be so bold as to send new wolves into Arek's territory without asking permission?

The wolves on the screen continued their destruction of the apartment. Both of them had claws out now and the slashed and crushed indiscriminately. Bolt winced when they smashed the TV, and if it weren't for the dire thoughts of betrayal on Arek's mind, he would have chuckled.

Bolt turned the laptop back so that it faced him. "Nothing exciting happens. They just keep getting angrier." He tapped on the computer. "I'm sending a screenshot to Justice to see if he knows them. And I'll widen the search for matching footage outside of the western region. If they're from another pack coalition and have ever been caught on camera somewhere, I'll find them."

"Start searching out east," Arek said, an awful feeling spreading through his body. Nicholai Novikov, the Eastern Packs Coalition's alpha, had started fighting the alphas of his neighboring packs to expand his territory. And he had married a dark witch.

"My thoughts exactly," Bolt said. "I'm already on it." He tapped the keyboard again. "And I'm checking traffic cameras to see where they went from here."

Arek paced the apartment while Bolt worked on the laptop. A few months ago, Novikov had tried to kidnap the girlfriend of billionaire Magnus Flink, a lone wolf in Denver.

He'd done so to force Flink to join the Eastern packs and thereby have to pay tithings to Novikov. Arek had been in Denver to warn Flink about Novikov's territory expansion and helped rescue Mina Parker, the girlfriend. She now worked for Arek's security business remotely by vetting his new clients. Magnus Flink technically still operated as a lone wolf but claimed ties with Arek's pack as a consultant. After the Denver incident, Novikov had lain low, and Arek had hoped that would be the end of it. His gut feeling told him that the alpha and his dark witch were behind this, though.

His cell phone vibrated in his pocket at the same time as Bolt's mobile beeped. Arek retrieved his device and checked the incoming message.

On the screen, Justice's message displayed, "Novikov's wolves." Short and to the point.

"Fuck," Arek said.

Bolt hadn't bother to check his phone. "It's as we suspected." He made it a statement and kept tapping the keyboard. "I have their car on camera. It's heading south."

Arek kept pacing, welcoming the rage that welled up inside him. Fucking Novikov.

Did he honestly think he could send wolves into Arek's territory and get away with it? Even worse, did he think he could send a disgraced witch to steal his medallion? "I want those wolves, and I want that woman." He growled.

"You'll get them." Bolt promised. After a few minutes, he stopped typing and looked up at Arek. "They're at a storage facility in San Mateo."

Arek strode to the door, his wolf so close to surface he knew his eyes had turned ice-blue. "We need to get those wolves," he growled. "And I want that woman."

CHAPTER 5

*L*aney desperately needed water, but paradoxically, she also needed to pee. However, the pain in her arms distracted her from both the pressure in her bladder and her dry throat.

She'd come to a few hours ago, her wrists tied together and looped over a hook that fastened in the ceiling. The man dressed in black had sat in a chair in front of her and laughed out loud when she awoke with a start and then scrambled to find her footage on the floor. The bastard had hung her just high enough to where her toes nudged the ground, but not enough to get traction so she could relieve her arms from taking the brunt of her weight.

Like a slab of slaughter on a meat hook.

After he's had enough amusement, the man had started their "conversation."

As she had suspected earlier, Laney had not enjoyed it.

Her throat still ached from screaming, and if it weren't for the pain in her arms, she'd probably whimper from the lacerations she had on her back. The bastard had whipped her, both with magic and an actual whip. The offending leather tool now lay in a corner of the room. The lone standing lamp by the opposite wall provided just enough light for her to see the multi-tail flail.

She wasn't sure how long the conversation had lasted because she'd passed out for a while. The man in black had not been pleased and threw cold water on her. She assumed it was water. It could have been magic for all she knew.

It had been cold. That's all Laney knew.

Considering how hot the temperature inside the room was right now, she almost wished for another cold dousing.

The man had left a few hours ago, perhaps. Keeping track of time proved difficult between the waves of pain that shuddered through her body. Someone had knocked on what Laney thought was a wall, but it turned out to be a shutter door that the man had opened and then stepped outside. There'd been a lot of shouting, and then whoever had come and the man both left. She remembered hearing two sets of footsteps. At first, she'd been relieved, but now she wondered if they'd left her here to die.

It seemed a sad way to end her life, hanging from a hook in the ceiling, slowly twisting in a circle, which gave her alternating views of a very sad lamp, a folding chair, and a whip.

Laney tried to pull herself up on the hook again. Maybe if she just lifted her body a little, she could kind of jump and slip off the hook. But it was no use. She didn't have enough strength left. *Should have done more crunches at the gym, lazy girl.* She chuckled, but it turned into a dry cough and just made her thirstier.

She'd screamed for help, but considering nobody came to her aid during the "conversation," she had no high hopes of attracting a rescuer. Besides, her broken voice didn't carry very far anyway.

She sniffed a little as a tear trailed down her cheek but

then defiantly blinked to dry her eyes. Wasting moisture was a bad idea when she was already so dehydrated.

A small scratching sound came from outside, and Laney held her breath to hear better. It sounded like claws scraping against metal.

Please, please, don't be rats.

She whimpered and then forced herself to be quiet. Compared to being eaten alive by rats, dying of dehydration and starvation now seemed desirable ways in which to leave this world.

Suddenly, the door flew open with a loud bang.

Laney blinked against a bright spotlight aimed at her eyes. It took her a little while to clear her vision, and when she did, she kept blinking because what she saw didn't make sense.

It had become night during the hours she'd been swinging on the hook. She welcomed the cool breeze wafting in from outside. Against the backdrop of the intense light from a building opposite and illuminated rain-spattered asphalt stood two wolves the size of small ponies. One, slate gray with a white blaze running from the tip of its nose to the forehead, watched her with cold ice-blue eyes. The other's pelt glimmered silver in the light. Its forest green gaze was as chilly as the other's.

The grey wolf stepped into the room.

Laney shook her head wildly. "No," she tried to scream, but it came out a hoarse whisper from her cracked lips. She'd rather be eaten by rats than torn apart by wild beasts.

The air around the wolf shimmered, and Arek Varg stood in its place. A very naked, very muscular Arek Varg.

Laney blinked again. Were fever dreams a sign of being close to the end?

"Dr. Marconi, I presume?" Varg asked.

Laney nodded, still staring, trying not to look lower than

his face. She was in a lot of pain. But this was a perfect fever dream, and she was curious about what her subconscious would create below Varg's waist.

He strode toward her and lifted his hands.

Laney couldn't help it. She flinched and whimpered, anticipating a blow.

Varg's eyes flashed, and he cursed under his breath. Moving slower, he turned her so that her side was to him. He supported her butt and hoisted her up with one arm. With the other, he lifted her off the hook.

As soon as Laney's feet touched the ground, she crumbled into a pile and couldn't help but cry out. Everything hurt.

Another curse left Varg's lips, this one a little louder. "Run and get the car," he told the other wolf.

It growled in response and took off.

Laney pushed against the floor with her bound hands to get off the floor but only managed to barely lift her head.

Varg slowly crouched down next to her and extended his hand.

She swallowed hard but managed not to flinch this time.

"I got you," he said and cupped her elbow.

With his help, Laney managed to get up on her knees. That was as much energy as she had right now. She licked her lips. "What are you doing here?" His grip on her elbow felt very real. This was obviously not a fever dream.

"I believe you have something that belongs to me." His now azure blue eyes flickered to a much lighter color and then back again. He tilted his head and studied her, a very wolf-like gesture.

She licked her lips. "About that." Laney didn't know how to continue. What could she say? "Someone set me up," she finally settled on.

"I very much doubt that," Varg said.

She bristled. "What do you think happened here? Do you

think I whip myself and then twirl around on meat hooks just for fun?"

He looked away for a beat, glancing up at the hook. "Maybe you were trying to take Novikov for more money, and he didn't like it."

"Who?" Laney asked.

"You're good." Varg smiled, but it wasn't a happy expression. "But you're not fooling me twice."

The sound of screeching tires came from down the row of storage units, and Varg quickly moved so that she was behind him. His shoulders tensed, and his fists clenched.

When an unobtrusive black sedan came into view, he relaxed and turned to face Laney. "Can you stand?"

She managed to get vertical with his help, but her legs wouldn't hold her when he let go. Varg scooped her up and carried her over to the car.

She considered protesting, but what was the point? Her body's weakness made it impossible to walk, or even stand, on her own. She hated being helpless.

The driver's side door opened, and a man dressed in grey sweats and a hoodie covering his head got out. Dark stubble graced his chiseled chin. He watched her with the same intensely green eyes that the silver wolf had, his gaze just as hostile as the beast's had been.

"Get the blanket from the trunk," Varg told him.

The other man sighed but did as asked and wrapped it around Laney. He then opened the rear door of the car. She huddled into the warm piece of fabric as Varg gently positioned her on the back seat. He stepped around the car, and when he came back in to view, he too wore sweats, but with a t-shirt. If she hadn't been distracted by pain, Laney would have mourned the disappearance of his fine body.

She held out her hands. "Can you cut me loose, please?"

Varg laughed. "Not a chance, witch." He closed the door in

her face and got in the driver's seat.

The other man slid into the passenger seat.

Varg watched her through the rearview mirror. His eye color had returned to ice blue. "You have until we get home to tell me where the medallion is."

Laney sighed. "What do you think I'm going to do if you release my hands? Zap you and run away? My legs don't work."

"I'm not taking any chances." Varg ignited the engine and started driving.

The other man spoke for the first time. "Good thinking. Witches are tricky."

Laney sighed again, but inwardly this time. She'd heard of shifters' prejudice against all forms of magic, but she thought most of them were more evolved than that. "There's nothing tricky about magic," she said. "It's another supernatural ability. Like shifting into a wolf, for example."

The two men in the front exchanged a look that spoke volumes about their opinions on comparing magic to shifting. They obviously disagreed.

Laney tried to pull the blanket more tightly around her, but it was hard with her bound hands. She met Varg's gaze in the mirror and held up her hands again.

He shook his head. "Start talking," he said.

So much for chivalry.

Laney took a deep breath. "I work for insurance companies to retrieve stolen artifacts," she began.

The man in the passenger seat twisted his body and faced her. "You mean you're a thief," he said in a cold voice. "Don't dress it up."

She sighed inwardly. This was going to be a long car ride.

At least she had the medallion as a bargaining chip. Hopefully, negotiations with the shifters would not involve torture.

$\mathcal{A}$rek studied his reluctant house guest from across the dinner table. She'd been put-out when they'd arrived at the pack house. Somehow, she'd thought he meant her apartment when he said he'd take her home. She still pouted about that.

Dr. Marconi sat very straight in her chair, probably because her back must hurt like hell. He'd sent the pack medical doctor up to the room to see to her injuries. The doctor said the lashes were severe but didn't need stitches. As long as they could keep them from being infected, Dr. Marconi should be okay. Arek's jaw clenched. That asshole Novikov had whipped her back to shreds. Sadistic bastard.

He'd suggested his guest take her meal in her room, but she'd refused and insisted on joining him for dinner. One thing he'd learned about Dr. Marconi so far, she was stubborn as hell. Despite being tortured by Novikov, she kept the whereabouts of the medallion quiet. Not that Arek would beat the information out of her, but she didn't know that.

"Is the food not to your liking," he asked as he chewed his own excellent steak.

His guest startled as if she'd been deep in thought and regarded him with striking amber-colored eyes. She picked up her fork and knife and cut a piece of the meat. "It's great," she said. "My compliments to the chef. I guess I'm just not very hungry." She wore sweats, and the size she'd chosen from the piles he had on hand whenever pack members needed a change of clothes after shifting, were a little too big.

"I'll let her know you enjoyed the meal, but you need to eat more," Arek said. "You've lost a lot of blood and need to replenish with both nutrition and liquids." He pointedly took a sip of his water glass.

She sighed but drank some water and then kept eating. "I still don't understand why I couldn't just go home. You know where I live now, so it's not like you couldn't keep tabs on me." She quirked an eyebrow. "Especially since you've hacked into my surveillance system." Bolt had shown her the footage of her destroyed apartment, but instead of being outraged over the damage, Dr. Marconi expressed anger over the fact that they could "spy" on her at any time "like some kind of perverts."

Arek smiled at the memory. His lieutenant had walked out in the middle of Dr. Marconi's tirade. She had not been pleased. If anything, it increased her indignation. "Why are you so set on returning when it's not safe? Until we catch the shifters that destroyed your place and neutralize Novikov, you are in danger, Dr. Marconi."

"Laney," she tilted her head, and red highlights glimmered as her wavy brown hair moved. "I asked you to call me Laney."

"There's also the small matter of returning my medallion, Laney." He emphasized her name but would keep thinking of her as Dr. Marconi. It was safer that way. The little witch already tempted and distracted him. He could afford neither with Novikov and his wolves running wild in Arek's territory.

A faint blush colored her honey-colored skin. "Yes, yes. The medallion," she muttered. "I've already apologized profusely about that. I told you, the man you think is Novikov set up a whole fake insurance company and gave me counterfeit paperwork."

Arek didn't quite believe that story, but something had obviously gone sour between her and Novikov. Whatever the reason, he couldn't just send her out there on her own. Justice and Bolt were out looking for the Eastern Packs Commanding Alpha and his shifters now. "I don't care why you stole it," he said. "Where is my talisman, and when will I have it back?"

She put down her cutlery and deliberately took her time chewing and swallowing. That amber gaze met his again. After he'd dealt with Novikov—and she'd return the Odin medallion—he'd like to seduce her just to see what those gorgeous eyes looked like when filled with passion. "Look," she said. "I have one bargain chip here, and it's that damn necklace. I'd be stupid to just give it up without some kind of guarantee that I'll make it out of this situation alive."

Gorgeous and smart. "And why would I think a thief would keep her bargain?" He chuckled. "For that matter, why do you think I'd feel obligated to honor any agreement with someone who stole from me?" She looked away and swallowed hard. Dr. Marconi wasn't as unafraid as she'd like him to think she was. Good. She should be wary of him.

She fiddled with the fork on the side of her plate. "You have a reputation of being an honest and fair man."

"Tell me where the medallion is, and I will treat you fairly."

A wry smile played on her lips. "I think I'll hold on to my bargaining chip a little bit longer. It's in a safe place."

He needed the amulet back, especially with Novikov running loose in his territory, but he'd play her game a little longer. He didn't relish having to force a woman. Besides, he had wolves re-searching her place now that the stench of dark magic should have faded. If the medallion were there, they'd find it. "Then we're at an impasse because you'll stay here until I get it back."

She scoffed. "What do you expect me to do while I'm here? I'll be bored out of my mind rattling around in this huge mansion." She gestured wildly, and he assumed the movement meant his whole house. It wasn't a mansion but sometimes pack members stayed with him for a while, so he needed extra bedrooms, like the one Dr. Marconi was currently occupying. Plus, Justin and Bolt had their quarters here. And his chef had insisted on a professional kitchen, both in terms of equipment and size. Plus, they needed a gym, of course, which had required an addition since the room that housed his collection of magical artifacts took up the entire basement. Okay, so it was a big house, but not a *mansion*.

"That's not my concern," he countered, but an idea that had brewed in his mind since they'd first gotten back to the house solidified. "Although, there might be something you can help me with."

She eyed him warily. "What?"

"Finish your meal, and I'll tell you."

She sighed again but picked up her fork and continued eating.

AREK UNLOCKED the door to the basement room that he thought of as "the vault" because of the lead shielding that encompassed the whole room.

Dr. Marconi fidgeted beside him. "Are you going to show me your dungeon?" Underneath her brave words, her voice shook with nervousness.

He leaned toward her, close enough where she could feel his breath on her skin. "Do you want me to show you my dungeon?" She smelled delicious. Like peaches and cream, he wanted to taste her skin. Yup, she was a dangerous temptation.

A deep flush crept up her neck and cheeks. "No," she sputtered.

Arek chuckled. He'd known she'd turn him down. He wouldn't have flirted with her if that hadn't been a guaranteed outcome. "This is where I keep my collection." He gestured for her to proceed him. "Depending on how you play your cards, I'll show you my dungeon later."

"I don't want to see your dungeon. I mean, I don't believe you have a—oh, wow." She stepped into the room and slowly turned in a circle. "This is amazing."

He looked around the space, trying to see it with her eyes. To an expert in magical artifacts, it would probably appear a treasure trove. To him, it was just storage for items that could hurt his wolves. Since he'd been alive for more than a century, the collection had grown quite a bit.

Dr. Marconi trailed her fingers along the shelves as she perused the items encased in various boxes and chests. Some of them as old as the items they contained. Most of them had attached placards with the name of the object, but not all of them. He had no idea what many of the items were, just that they contained magic and could hurt a shifter.

"How have you kept this a secret?" Dr. Marconi whispered. "All magical relics are supposed to be reported to a university so they can catalog it."

Arek frowned. Maybe it had been a mistake showing her this. "Says who?"

She turned to face him. "Says the Witch and Mage council."

He dismissed her words with a hand gesture. "I don't answer to them."

She opened her mouth but then closed it again. "I suppose not," she finally said with a little chuckle. Her eyes glittered. "Oh man, they'd be so pissed if they'd find out about the treasures you keep here."

"Who would tell them?" An edge crept into his voice.

Dr. Marconi did that head tilt again. "Well, I sure won't. I owe no loyalty to them. Quite the opposite." She stepped up to one of the shelves. "Is that an Arminian gold sacrificial dagger?" Leaning closer, a sigh escaped her lips. "Ah, man. That must be a thousand years old." She clenched her fists as if to keep from touching the item. "It's exquisite."

Arek shrugged. "I have no idea." The item was one that didn't have a description.

His guest turned toward him again. "Why are you showing me all of this?"

"You said you wanted to have something to do while you were here. I need all of these cataloged."

"You have all these treasures, but you haven't kept a record?" Incredulity laced her voice.

He looked around the room. "There are some ledgers somewhere, but I need a proper database created."

Dr. Marconi stared at him, her mouth opening and closing. "You're serious," she finally choked out. "You have no idea what's actually in here." She swept out with her hand, "or, whether they are stored safely?"

"It hasn't been a priority to keep track," Arek said, feeling vaguely guilty and pissed off about that. "I've been busy with other stuff."

"And you want me to catalog all of these items. I get to examine them." Her eyes grew big. "All of them."

He nodded. "If you want to."

She stepped deeper into the room, walking along the shelves at a clip. "Okay, I need a laptop, a crapload of salt, and a big tank of water."

Arek grinned, so much for being bored while stayed with him. He'd found the perfect way to distract the little witch while he searched for the medallion and dealt with Novikov.

After that, he would see about getting to know Dr. Marconi a little better. Preferably in bed. Her wounds had to heal first, so he had some time.

CHAPTER 7

*L*aney had just finished her shower when there was a knock on the door to the enormous suite where she'd spent the night. She circumvented a jetted tub big enough for four people to reach the door where a bathrobe hung. She knew Varg was wealthy, but the scale of his fortune had not hit home until she'd seen part of his house. Bolt was supposed to give her a tour of the rest this morning, and judging from the knock on the door, he was early.

She pulled on the robe and winced as the soft terrycloth touched her abused back. "Just a minute," she called, frantically toweling her hair as she walked to get the door. She belted her robe more securely and opened the door to find, just as expected, Bolt on the other side. They'd agreed to meet first thing in the morning, but she thought that meant that she would at least have a chance to take a shower and eat breakfast first. "You're too early," she said in the way of greeting.

"It was supposed to be first thing," Bolt answered, stepping into the suite without being asked. He carried a tray with him and went straight to deposit it on top of the polished marble-topped side table in the sitting room. Obviously, he'd been in this suite before or one just like it. "I brought breakfast," he said, gesturing to the tray and grabbed one of the plates covered with a silver dome and sat down at the small dining table that was just as polished and made of just as heavy wood as the rest of the furnishings in the suite.

"Good morning to you too," Laney said and lifted the cover on the remaining plate. Eggs Benedict with baby spinach and a mountain of fresh fruit greeted her. She took a deep breath, appreciating the tantalizing aroma of the food. "This smells heavenly."

Bolt made a sound somewhere between a snort and a laugh.

"What," Laney asked as he grabbed a rolled-up cloth napkin with silverware and carried her plate to the table.

"It just always amazes me how humans can't smell anything until they already see what it is." Bolt shoveled eggs and hollandaise sauce into his mouth like someone would pull his plate away at any minute. His plate had four muffins and eggs, compared to her two. Instead of fresh fruit, it was piled high with hash browns. Apparently, there were non-shifter portions and shifter portions in this house.

"No potatoes for me?" Laney asked. The hash browns would taste really good with the hollandaise sauce.

He stopped a loaded fork midair and gave her a surprised look. "Did you want some?" He lifted his dish, ready to shovel some of his hash browns onto her plate.

"I'll trade you some fruit," she said.

He looked at her plate for a moment. "Nah," he said finally, shoveling about a third of his potatoes on her plate. "I'm good without any of that stuff."

"Any of that stuff?" Laney asked. "Like fruit and vegetables?"

Bolt nodded. "Not enough calories per weight for a shifter. Especially after a shift."

"You just shifted?"

He paused for a beat and looked away. "Well, I went for a morning run," he finally said.

Laney looked out the wall of floor-to-ceiling windows and French doors that led out to a balcony. She'd noticed the spectacular view of Bonita Cove from the bedroom window when she first got up. On the way to Arek's house, she hadn't paid much attention to its location, but they were obviously in the Marin Headlands somewhere. On the other side of the Golden Gate Bridge from the city. "I've hiked up here several times and never noticed buildings here. I thought this was protected land. How did Varg get building permits?"

Bolt gestured toward the window with his fork. "This building has been here since before the state bought up the land. It's been pack land forever. The first alpha who built a cabin on this site negotiated with the people who has the real claim to the land, the Coastal Miwok."

Laney sat back. "The wolves have been here since before the English and Spanish arrived?" That was a long freaking time.

"The wolves lived in harmony with the original people and tried to fight the English and the Spanish. Many of the wolves had Miwok true mates." Bolt kept eating.

"True mates?"

He put down his fork. "A wolf's mate for life. You don't know very much about shifters, do you?"

Laney shook her head. "I used to work at the university's magical artifacts department and curated their museum—"

"I know, Bolt interrupted."

Laney stopped. Of course, he knew. They must have researched her to find her address. Which meant the wolves knew about her resigning in disgrace, as well. She took a deep breath and continued, ignoring the interruption. "And some of my colleagues were shifters, but they didn't socialize much with the mages and witches." Some of them had been outright rude and refused to serve on committees with anyone who had magical abilities.

"Makes sense." Bolt nodded.

"How does that make sense? Why the prejudice against my kind?" She knew shifters were averse to magic, but the ability to shift was just another side to having any magical ability.

"In my case, I have a good reason," Bolt muttered and shoveled in the last of his food.

Laney waited, but apparently, that was all the wolf would share. She decided to change the topic. "Did you grow up in this pack?" Learning more about Varg and his pack would be helpful.

"No," Bolt said, scraping his plate and looking at what remained on hers. "Are you done with breakfast?"

She pushed the plate over to him, and he dug in but pushed the fruit to the side. "Where did you grow up then?"

"I have no idea." Laney made a surprised sound, and Bolt looked up from his plate. "Arek found Justice and me in the fighting pits. I have no memory of my life before that."

She swallowed a gasp. The brutal world of underground prizefighting had a dark reputation of indentured combatants that had to fight to earn their freedom. "What's your earliest memory then?"

He studied her for a beat. "I was about twelve, and someone, maybe a parent, told me I had to listen to the fight master from now on."

This time she couldn't keep her gasp from escaping. "Your parents sold you to the fighting pits?"

Bolt shrugged. "It happens to a lot of shifter kids. Sometimes because their parents need money. Sometimes because they don't know how to handle a kid who turns into a preda-tory animal at inopportune times." She opened her mouth to ask more, but he stood and gathered their dishes. "That's enough chitchat. Let's get going." He dumped their plates back on the tray with enough noise that it was clear the discussion about his past was closed and walked toward the door of the suite.

Laney cleared her throat. "Um, I need to get dressed first."

He turned around and looked at her as if he'd not even noticed her wet hair, robe, or dripping towel draped over her shoulders. "Oh. How long will that take?"

She sighed and walked through to the bedroom and en suite bathroom. "As long as it takes," she said over her shoulder and closed the door between them.

Laney quickly straightened the sheets on the bed and pulled up the bed cover before piling the pillows she'd thrown on the floor the night before on top of the bedding. The mattress had been soft enough to cradle her sore body but firm enough to relax her cramped back. The tread count of the sheets was several digits higher than she could afford for herself.

She'd always appreciated quality stuff, but the furnishings that Arek Varg had in his house were leagues above what she had treated herself with when she outfitted her apartment in Bernal Heights.

The thought of all her nice furniture smashed to pieces made her sigh. It would take a big chunk out of her savings to buy new stuff for her place. And not just furniture, but dishes, clothes, and bedding. It was as if she was starting from scratch.

She went into the bathroom to brush the snarls out of her hair. The granite-covered vanity was filled with toiletries, all packed in sanitized bags. She'd found a brush, a hairdryer, even some styling products in one of the cabinets. There was even some unopened makeup. Either Arek Varg didn't want company in his bed after he'd seduced someone, or he had a lot of overnight visitors staying with him. Maybe a combination of both.

Laney opened a fresh toothbrush, squeezed some paste out from a travel-size tube, and began cleaning her teeth.

The idea of starting over fresh didn't hurt as much emotionally as financially. She'd bought all her stuff when she first started at the university. Back then, as a revered academic with a busy social life, she'd often entertained in her apartment. Not so much since her fall from grace. Maybe she should even think about getting a smaller place. She didn't need much more than a studio, and since rents in San Francisco were sky high, it would be a good idea to cut back on that expense. Especially now that it didn't look like she was going to get paid for retrieving the medallion.

She spat and rinsed. The reflection looking back at her in the mirror didn't look too bad considering she'd spent most of yesterday hanging from a meat hook. Her arms were still sore and her back hurt like hell. There was some bruising underneath her eyes, but other than that, she looked okay from her ordeal. The bathrobe pulled a little on her wounds as she peeled it off and hung it on the back of the bathroom door. She turned so she could see her back in the mirror. Whatever the stuff was that the pack's doctor had slathered on her gashes, it had helped. They were still red, but none of them bled anymore, and they looked clean and healthy. Being a witch with ties to earthbound materials also gave her the advantage of accelerated healing.

She padded naked into the bedroom and opened the big armoire that matched the bed's dark wood. Inside were piles of sweats, yoga pants, and t-shirts in various colors and sizes, as well as cotton panties and sports bras. She chose a deep blue t-shirt that made her think of Varg's eyes and a pair of light grey yoga pants. On her feet, she put fresh crew socks and then laced up the brand new black and blue trainers she'd found in her size the night before.

She returned to the bathroom and dug out a hair fastener that she used to put her still wet hair in a ponytail. That would have to do.

Bolt's first words to her when she stepped out of the bedroom were, "About time."

Laney smiled. In total, she'd been away for ten minutes.

"You don't have a girlfriend, do you?"

He gave her a startled look. "What does that have to do with anything?"

She chuckled. "Nothing. Maybe you prefer boyfriends?"

"Why do you want to know?" He eyed her suspiciously. "Are you flirting with me? I'm not interested in witches. Male or female."

Laney burst out laughing. "I'm not hitting on you, but that's good to know."

"Look, do you want this tour or not?" Bolt sounded irritated.

"Yes," Laney answered. The faster she learned the house's layout, the quicker she could figure out how to get the hell out of here. Although, now that Varg had shown her his treasure trove, she wasn't in as much of a hurry to escape.

The wolf had no idea what priceless artifacts he'd collected over the years, and she couldn't wait to examine and study them all.

Something deep inside her stirred.

Something she'd suppressed for a long time.

For the first time in almost two years, she felt a familiar hunger that she had missed.

A desire to search for clues of what had once been and how it helped build today's cultures.

She couldn't wait to get back down in that basement.

CHAPTER 8

*A*rek logged out of the video conference software and closed down his laptop. The discussion with the other alphas in the Western Packs Coalition had gone okay. About as well as expected, considering the purpose of the special call was to inform them that an intruder was in their territory. The coalition met monthly, and Arek loathed the obligation because although the wolves understood the necessity of being in a coalition, they were all alphas. Getting them to agree on anything could be exhausting. However, today's call had given them a common enemy, and the possibility of a good fight had them united. Well, as united as a bunch of domineering wolves could be. They had agreed to oust the interloper, precisely what that would look like had not been agreed on. Some of them called for a public execution. Others wanted to know Novikov's motivation before they acted.

Arek just wanted the Russian and his wolves out of the Bay Area pack territory.

He shouldn't complain about the alphas he worked with,

though. Compared to the politics of some of the other coalitions, the Western Pack's was relatively frictionless. There had been one occasion where a younger wolf tried to instigate infighting within the coalition to advance his standing within the packs, but the local alpha in charge had snuffed out the rebellion before anything serious became of it.

For the most part, the Western Packs Coalition local alphas saw the benefits of having a union because it discouraged fighting over territories and resources while giving access to a larger number of fighting wolves and weapons when facing an outside enemy.

Nora Bretagne, the legal advisor of his pack, entered the office. "I researched the travel records as you requested," she said. Except for Bolt, Nora was the best hacker of his pack. She combined those skills with a brilliant strategic mind, and Arek often thought of her as his secret weapon. As a woman, she was often underestimated in the macho wolf culture and knew how to use that to her advantage. "There is no Nicholai Novikov traveling to the western states in the last six months."

Arek sighed. "It was worth a try, though." He'd asked Nora to check all modes of travel to California or neighboring states, just in case Novikov drove the last part of the journey to avoid detection. "The bastard is probably traveling under an assumed name. Can we check security film from airports and run facial recognition?"

"Not done yet." Nora held up a hand, interrupting him. They'd known each other for a long time, and she treated him as a brother. Sometimes she became overly familiar but rarely disrespectful. He didn't mind. Arek preferred to have people who called him on his shit, whether he wanted them to or not. "I also checked hotels and house rentals in Northern California to see if anyone by that name had checked in or rented a place." She smiled. "I'm not just a pretty face, you know."

Arek returned her grin. Nora's features were striking, and both men and women often stopped to stare because her mere presence commanded attention. However, she thought their attention was due to a large scar that ran from the corner of her right brow, across her eye, and down to the top of her lip. To him, it marked her a warrior, but Nora often used self-deprecating humor to draw attention to the scar as a defense mechanism. "Your face is one of the prettiest I know," he said, "but your amazing brain is what I fell in love with." Arek grinned at her.

She laughed. "Oh please, I'm not one of your conquests. Save the flattery and the killer smile for someone it will work on."

Arek chuckled. "Fine, tell me what you found."

"No Novikovs are staying in the Bay Area or the immediately adjacent regions." Nora looked down at a tablet in her hand. "However, I did find an Inessa Aslanova and Iakov Aslanov at a DoubleTree hotel in Modesto."

"Inessa is the name of Novikov's new wife," Arek said.

Nora smiled again. "I know. And after doing some digging, which took a while because she's erased a lot of personal data, but not even dark magic can erase all cyber tracks, I managed to find out that Aslanova is her mother's last name."

"So, her maiden name?"

"No, her maiden name is her father's last name, and Inessa used the female version, Butosova, before she married Novikov. Her brother, however, has always used the male version of their mother's last name."

"Her brother?" Arek echoed. "And female and male last names?

Nora nodded. "Russian last names have different endings

depending on whether the person is male or female. Very backwoods and binary specific, I know." She shook her head. "But my point is, there are two dark magic siblings in our territory, Inessa and Iakov."

"Oh, fuck."

"My sentiments exactly," Nora said. "Nicholai may not even be here. He sent his wife and brother-in-law instead."

Arek growled. "Doesn't matter. He's still trespassing uninvited on pack territory."

Nora tapped the tablet. "You may have some problems with that."

"What are you talking about?"

"Well, according to the Pack Directives that were drawn up when the coalitions formed, any wolf of an outside pack must ask permission from the Commanding Alpha before entering a territory and should also inform the local pack alpha of them being in the area. However, Nicholai could claim that since Inessa and Iakov are not wolves, the rules do not apply."

"That's bullshit." Arek banged his fist on the table. "Everyone knows it applies to all pack members of an outside pack. We discussed the law's intent when that rogue wolf and his human true mate infringed on the Central Packs' territory. The wolf argued that the rules didn't apply to his mate since she wasn't a wolf, but the intent of the law determined the outcome of the case."

Nora nodded. "Yes, there was much discussion. But nobody updated the Pack Directives, so the original wording of the law remains 'wolf.' The Eastern Packs' lawyer was supposed to update the documents to say 'member' instead. But when he had an accident and died, it never happened."

Arek sighed. "An accident orchestrated by Nick Novikov, no doubt."

"Very likely," Nora agreed. "The lawyer worked for the

previous alpha that Novikov challenged and killed, and refused to step down when the regime changed."

Fucking politics. Fucking Eastern Packs ambitious alpha. "Is there a way to keep track of the dark witch and her brother?"

"I've reached out to some contacts in the Sacramento pack. They're on their way to Modesto to hopefully find the siblings' vehicle and install a tracker." She shrugged. "I wouldn't get my hopes up, though. The two of them must know that you'll want to put surveillance on them once you discover they're here."

"What about the two wolves that we caught on camera in Dr. Marconi's apartment?"

Nora sighed. "I don't have any information on them other than that they are members of Novikov's pack. They seem to have vanished after they broke into Dr. Marconi's apartment." She hugged the tablet to her. "By the way, what are you going to do about her?"

"What do you mean?"

"You can't just imprison her and keep her under house arrest. The Witch and Mage Council will eventually find out and insist you either take legal action against her or let her go."

Spoken just like a lawyer, but Arek doubted the council would involve themselves much in Dr. Marconi's case. They seemed to have washed their hands of her when they made her resign from her university and museum posts. "She's not a prisoner. She can leave anytime she wants. All she has to do is give me the medallion?"

Nora's eyebrows shot to the top of her forehead. "Have you told her that?"

Of course, he hadn't told her that. It would defeat the purpose of having her scared enough to give up the medallion. Although, that had kind of backfired. The good doctor seemed to think she had to hold on to the artifact for protection from him. "She knows," he lied to Nora.

"Mm-hm," she answered, one eyebrow quirked. He avoided her knowing gaze. Maybe it wasn't all that good to have people working for him that could call his bullshit. Nora waved her hand. "Anyway, how about you show her a picture of Inessa and Iakov? It could have been either of them that held her captive in the storage facility. I'm sure Inessa can take on a male form." She handed him a printout. In the image, a man and a woman in evening wear smiled at a camera. It looked like they were at some kind of society function. Both of them were tall and icy-blond. They looked remarkably alike.

"Are they twins," Arek asked?

Nora shook her head. "No, Inessa is two years older. But, of course, one of the perks of being a dark witch, or mage, is that you don't age."

"Until the magic claims its prize." Arek countered. Every time a practitioner performed a dark magic spell or rite, they lost part of their humanity. Old folklore said a stain was put upon their soul. Eventually, there was no humanity left, and the mage or witch either withered and died—soulless—or, in some rare cases, became a ravenous beast that hunted and devoured all other creatures, but especially supernatural beings.

He shook himself out of those dark thoughts. "Let's go find Dr. Marconi and show her this picture. I want you to meet her and tell me what you think of her."

"I already like her," Nora said as she walked out of the office. "I heard her talking to Bolt when they passed my office during their house tour. She's driving him mad with all her questions."

Arek chuckled. One of the reasons he'd asked Bolt to do

the tour was because he knew the tight-lipped wolf wouldn't share information he shouldn't.

Also, the only other person he'd trust with Dr. Marconi, Justice, was currently searching her apartment again, looking for where she'd hid the medallion.

CHAPTER 9

*L*aney never wanted to leave the spectacular sunroom on the second floor. Jutting out of the mansion corner, it had only a few feet of solid ceiling where the room abutted the house. The rest of the roof, and the walls, were made entirely of glass. She could spend days just watching the view from here. To the west, Bonita Cove's beaches framed the half-circle bay that ended in the skinny Point Bonita peninsula and its lone lighthouse. Beyond that, the blue waters of the Pacific Ocean stretched until the horizon. A straight line from where she currently lay curled up on a day lounger, except for a few atolls, the next solid landfall would be Japan. This, of course, was true from any point in San Francisco, but the impact of all that water hit harder here when she saw it stretched out for miles and miles.

She twisted so she could look out to the east. The Golden Gate Bridge rose majestically out of a fog bank, its color contrasting dramatically with the fog's grey and the dark blue of the swirling waters underneath. The landmark seemed to claim its place with such confidence that Laney couldn't even imagine that it hadn't always been there. The fact that it was less than a hundred years old seemed impossible. Everything on the north side of the bridge, where she was now, would have been so isolated before the bridge's completion.

Laney adjusted her position again and looked straight ahead out the windows. She had to stretch her neck a little to see the end of Point Diablo and the small white shack that held the blinking light warning incoming ships of the protruding land hazard.

"Are you done yet?" Bolt wanted to know. He stood next to Laney's lounger despite that there were several equally comfortable loungers and chairs on which he could rest his butt. Instead, he hovered over her, his arms crossed and a miserable frown on his face.

"Nope." She gestured toward the cozy furniture scattered around the room. "Why don't you rest for a while. Tell me some more about the pack and how it works?" Potted palms and other large plants thrived in the sunlit room. How could he not want to just relax for a bit in the beautiful space?

Bolt remained standing, and the furrows above his brows deepened. "I haven't told you anything about how the pack works."

"Exactly," Laney said. She must have asked a hundred questions during their house tour, and except for details about how the exercise equipment in the gym worked, Bolt had divulged nothing useful. "I'm supposed to work with the Varg's artifacts, but I don't know anything about pack customs or rules."

"None of the items in the basement come from the pack." Bolt rubbed his palm over the short stubble on top of his head.

"How do you know?"

"Because the pack doesn't deal with magic. Arek's collection is contained in the basement to keep the artifacts from being used against shifters."

Laney tilted her head so she could better watch Bolt's face without the sun in her eyes. "But the Odin medallion has power."

He stilled and narrowed his eyes. "No, it doesn't."

She felt like saying, "does too," but decided the reply a little too childish. "I felt it when I touched it."

Bolt took a menacing step forward and leaned over her, his face close to hers. "Whatever you think you felt. I would advise you to keep that detail to yourself."

A chill slid down Laney's spine, but not because Bolt scared her. He looked menacing, but she didn't think he'd hurt her without physical provocation. The cold sliver came from finally discovering something useful. Maybe she could use something else to bargain with because she would eventually have to give him back the necklace. She straightened in her seat and stared right back at the wolf. "And if I don't?"

"What's going on here?" Arek Varg asked from the doorway, hand on hips. The cream cable-knit sweater that perfectly molded to his chest looked thin yet warm. Another piece of expensive clothing. His piercing blue eyes were aimed at Laney, but she couldn't interpret their expression.

Behind the alpha stood a tall woman with flaming red hair styled in a chin-length bob. Her hand covered her mouth, and from the delight glittering in her eyes, it was an attempt at hiding a smile. A white line ran from her brow to the top of her lip, but it detracted nothing from her gorgeous face.

Bolt straightened and took a step back. He looked at Laney and shook his head in annoyance. "Just don't," he said. He turned toward the door. "Boss, may I please be excused from this woman? Odin, forgive me, but I am way past the limit of my patience." Before the alpha could answer, Bolt walked out of the room.

Varg opened his mouth to say something but closed it again. He looked at Laney again. "What did you do to him?"

"Nothing," Laney answered. "I've been the perfect guest the whole day. If anything, he's the one whose lacking as a tour guide, refusing to answer even the most mundane questions."

The tall woman's shoulders shook, and she snorted. She tried to cover it up with a cough but gave up and laughed out loud. Grabbing a piece of paper that Varg had in his hand, she strode over to where Laney sat. "I'm Nora," she said, "the pack's lawyer. Could you please take a look at this picture and tell me if you recognize anyone?" She sat in a chair next to Laney's and handed over the sheet.

Laney looked at the striking blond couple in the image. "They look like they are related. Who are they?"

"You don't know them?" Varg asked, watching her intensely. He'd walked over so quietly. She hadn't noticed him move. Now his muscular denim-covered thigh so close to her face proved distractive.

"The woman looks kind of familiar," Laney studied the picture more closely. "But I can't place her. What's her name?"

" Inessa Novikov, but you may know her better as Inessa Butosova, her maiden name," Nora said.

Butosova was familiar, but not in a good way. Laney frowned. "She's a dark witch. Like, really dark, and really bad news. The Witches and Mage Council has a whole team working on keeping magical artifacts out of her hands. She seems to have unlimited resources to purchase them at auctions."

Varg nodded. "She's now married to the Russian American alpha who commands the Eastern Pack. She and her brother are here on the west coast. We think one of them is your abductor."

Laney looked at the picture again. "I don't think it was Inessa, but maybe the man. He has the right height and build. Inessa could indeed have posed as male. I just have an impression of it being an actual male." She swallowed, not wanting to think about those hours she'd been hanging on the meat hook. "He kept distorting his features, though. So, it's only my gut feeling telling me it's a man. That and the fact that he had a broken nose. Every one of his shifting faces had that feature in common." She looked back at the picture again and pointed at the guy's face. "This guy's nose is crooked."

"I am almost certain Iakov is our guy." Nora sounded excited. "Nick Novikov does not have a broken nose."

A phone rang, and from his pocket, Varg fished out a mobile. "Yeah." He listened to the person on the other end and nodded a few times, and then his amused blue eyes caught Laney's gaze. "Justice wants to know what the combination is to the safe he found underneath the floorboards in your apartment."

How the fuck had they found her hiding spot? She'd warded that location with an obfuscation incantation several times over. "I have no idea what you're talking about," she tried but knew she wouldn't get away with it as soon as the words left her lips.

"Did you hear that?" Varg asked into the phone. Nora had her hand in front of her mouth, and her shoulders shook again. The alpha wolf held out the phone to Laney. "He wants to talk to you."

She sighed but took the phone. "Hello?"

"You alright, Luv?" Justice asked but didn't wait for an answer, "Just need to know if you want to give me the combination over the phone so I can open the safe here? Or should

I rip it out of the floor and take it to you? Trouble is, I may do a bit of damage if I have to move it." *Shit. Shit. Shit.* She tried to think of a way out of the situation, but there wasn't one. Varg watched her with a smile playing on his lips. She wanted to stick her tongue out at him. "Still there, Luv?" the Brit asked on the phone line.

"Look," Laney finally said. "You can't open it without me, and you can't move it without me."

"Pretty sure I can," Justice said. "I'm extremely strong."

She sighed. Dumb wolf thought brawn was the answer to everything. "The safe is warded with a kill incantation. If you try to open it without me present, or if you try to move it, you'll trigger the spell." The wolves were adversaries, but that didn't mean she wanted to cause Justice's death.

Nora took a deep breath, and Varg growled.

On the line, Justice just chuckled. "Clever girl. Well, you better get over here and open it for me, then."

Laney handed the phone back to Varg. "This isn't over," she told him, but her heart sank. She'd lost her strongest bargaining chip, but maybe she could still use the fact that the wolves didn't want anyone to know about the medallion's magical powers.

His eyes were cold as they met hers. "You almost killed my lieutenant."

She squared her shoulders. "No, I didn't. You almost got him killed by sending over to snoop at my apartment without asking permission."

"I don't remember you asking for permission when you stole the Odin medallion." He leaned over her, his eyes never leaving hers. The air crackled between them with anger and something more.

The air was suddenly too thick to enter her lungs properly. "What's so special about the medallion anyway?" The words spilled out of her mouth on a breath of air.

Varg's pupils widened as he focused on her lips. Her lungs stopped working altogether.

Nora cleared her throat.

Varg blinked and took a step back. "Let's go," he said over his shoulder as he walked out of the room.

Laney shook her head and had to force her shoulders to relax before she could get up from the lounger. Nora shot her an amused look and then followed Varg.

That moment did not need to be repeated, ever.

If Stockholm syndrome was when a victim sympathized with their capturer's cause, what did you call wanting to jump your jailer's bones?

CHAPTER 10

*A*rek looked around Dr. Marconi's apartment. The devastation didn't look any different from the last time he had visited, but this time, the place's owner was with him. She'd seen the wreckage through the video feed that Bolt had shown her, but experiencing it in person affected her emotionally. Her defiant behavior during their confrontation in the sunroom had disappeared.

Tears had welled up when they first walked into her wrecked home. She'd quickly blinked them away. He'd wanted to hug her, but after the sizzling attraction he'd felt for her when they argued, he needed to keep his hands well away from her.

Arek tried not to think about that if Dr. Marconi had less of a conscience, his enforcer would be dead by now. It hadn't occurred to him or Justice, but of course, a witch would ward her hiding place. The pack was ill-prepared to deal with a regular magic practitioner. They would need a lot more training and a lot more information before confronting Inessa Novikov and her brother. He needed to convince Dr. Marconi to stay at the Pack House and help them prepare.

She walked through the apartment, her eyes wide and her hand gripping her throat. Now and then, she'd stop and study something on the floor before continuing on her walk-through. Arek didn't want to rush her, but the longer they stayed here, the itchier he became. Sacramento's wolves had not been able to locate the dark magic siblings' car, and they were currently not at their Modesto hotel. None of them were safe until somebody had eyes on them. The safe that Justice had located was hidden beneath the floor under where her bed had stood before the two Eastern Pack wolves destroyed it.

His enforcer cleared his throat. "You alright, Luv?" he asked Dr. Marconi.

She took a while before she turned to face him. "Yeah," she finally said, gesturing toward the floor littered with debris. "I just didn't know it was this bad." She hiccupped but then squared her shoulders. "Right, the safe." She walked toward the bedroom. Arek and Justice followed.

Dr. Marconi kneeled on the floor next to where Justice had pried open the floorboards. Underneath was a black iron door with a keypad. "I'll open the safe," she said, "but I want your word that you will only take the medallion and leave the rest of the content with me."

Justice looked at Arek, one eyebrow raised. Arek nodded. "As long as there is nothing else inside the safe that belongs to a wolf pack, you can keep the content." He didn't add that neither Dr. Marconi nor whatever else was in the safe would be left in this apartment. The woman argued about every-thing, so he'd leave this confrontation for later.

She placed both hands on the floor next to the hole and closed her eyes. The air around her shimmered, and the flooring underneath rippled in smooth waves. She didn't make a sound, yet Arek heard chanting and drums as if very far away. He looked over at Justice, but his enforcer was staring at Dr. Marconi, leaning forward as if she was pulling him toward her with invisible strings. Her hands left the floor and twisted gracefully in the air. A stream of sand floated up from the safe, arranging itself in a thin stream that flowed into a pile on the floor, as if inside an invisible hourglass.

After a few minutes, the sand stopped, and Dr. Marconi sat back on her heels. "All done," she said.

"What is that?" Justice pointed at the cone of sand. "Magical dust?"

Dr. Marconi smiled. "I'm an earthbound witch. My magic works best on non-manmade materials. Enchanting the metal of the safe was too obvious. Also, I couldn't come up with one spell that effectively stopped someone from opening the safe and moving it. So, I packed the hole with warded sand before I lowered the safe into it.

"So, you made your own magical Semtex." Justice gripped his neck and grinned. "Fucking clever girl. Can you teach me to do that?"

She tilted her head. "Do you have any earthbound powers? Do you feel drawn to certain rocks or trees?"

"Can't say I ever noticed anything like that, no." His enforcer shook his head. "But let's get on with it, then. Crack that safe open, Luv. Arek wants his Odin medallion."

Dr. Marconi keyed in a code, twisted the handle on the safe, and swung open the door on silent hinges. She reached inside and took out a black velvet pouch. Arek immediately felt a familiar pull. His medallion was inside. She stood and walked over to him. "I'm sorry about taking this from you. I truly was set up."

He nodded, took the pouch from her, and retrieved the Odin artifact. It hung on a broken platinum chain.

"Oh," she said, reaching for the chain. When Arek instinctively swung it away from him, she cried out, "I can fix it."

He slowly handed it back to her. "Touch only the chain." She may have kept Justice from getting hurt, but that didn't mean he trusted her.

She rolled her eyes but did as he asked. Holding the two broken pieces of the chain together in one hand, she stroked a fingertip across the breakage, and the links of the chain twisted themselves together again. He studied the location of the break closely but couldn't see anything differentiating those links from the others.

"Thank you," he said. Although why he expressed gratitude when she was the one who had broken the thing in the first place, he didn't know.

Dr. Marconi reached into the safe again and took out a small leather dossier. "Okay then." She looked at them expectantly. "I guess this is where we say goodbye."

Fat chance. Arek fastened the chain around his neck. "What's in there, and where are you going to go?"

She waved the small folder in the air and looked around the apartment. "Cash and my passport, plus an emergency credit card. I guess I'll stay at a hotel for a few days until I clean this up and get some furniture in."

Justice shook his head. "You can't stay here. Even if this place wasn't a wreck, you got two deranged dark mages after you and their mangy wolves."

Dr. Marconi paled. "But I don't have the medallion anymore. Why would they still want to hurt me?"

"They don't know that," Arek said.

"And even if they did, they don't care," Justice added. "You got away from them before they could finish the job. You're a liability, Luv."

"Finish the job?"

"Expire you," his enforcer clarified. "They can't be sure you won't be able to identify them."

Her face turned even paler. "So, I was right. That meat

hook was supposed to be my final destination. She glanced around the apartment again. "I'll have to lay low for a while then. Maybe break my lease and get a new place."

Arek put his hand on her shoulder. "They'd still be able to find you, even if you left town. What you need is protection." He hoped she'd come to the correct conclusion on her own.

"I don't have anyone—," she stopped and swallowed. "I don't know how to—," she shook her head. "You want me to come back with you."

"That's a great idea," Justice said, clapping his hands once. "Let's get the fuck out of here before them deranged siblings or their wolves show up."

Dr. Marconi shook her head again. "No, I can't do that."

"Why not?" Arek asked at the same time as Justice said, "Where else are you going to go?"

"I can't just freeload off you. I need to get another insurance retrieval contract. Once I have some disposable cash, I'll have more options."

He sighed inwardly. Why did she have to make things so complicated? "You already have a great option. I already offered you a job."

She frowned. "You still want me to catalog your collection?"

"Of course." That and helping him prepare his wolves to take out the dark magic siblings. But that would be a later discussion.

She opened her mouth to say something, probably a protest of some sort, but Justice grabbed her shoulders and propelled her out of the apartment. "That's settled, then," he said. "Let's discuss the details on the way back to the Pack House." He grinned at Arek over his shoulder. "If I were you, Doctor, I'd negotiate a big salary with smashing benefits."

Great, now his enforcer was working for the witch.

* * *

AREK WALKED Dr. Marconi to her suite in the Pack House. She'd been quiet in the car back, despite him trying to pull her into a conversation. "Are you alright?" he asked as they reached her door.

She shrugged. "I will be. The live experience of my destroyed apartment—my destroyed life—affected me more than I thought it would."

He touched her shoulder and turned her around to face him. "Your life is not destroyed. Those were just things."

Her cognac-colored eyes stared up at him, and her lips parted.

He'd meant only to give her a hug for comfort, but now he couldn't stop staring at her mouth. Her tongue darted out and touched her bottom lip.

The wolf inside him growled in appreciation. *We like*, it whispered to him.

She reached up and traced a fingertip across his lips. "Soft," she whispered. "Just like I thought."

Mine, the wolf roared. *Ours*.

Arek could no longer resist the pull. He leaned down, his hand sliding from her shoulder down her back, pressing her against him. He buried his other hand in her glorious hair, and he crushed his lips against hers.

A moan escaped her lips, and he slipped his tongue inside her mouth. Tasting, devouring.

Claim mate, Wolf growled, the sound reverberating through Arek's chest.

CHAPTER 11

*L*aney grabbed the collar of Varg's shirt, pulling him closer. His lips were soft but firm against hers. As his tongue danced with hers, every nerve ending in her body shuddered in delight.

She laced her fingers behind his neck, pressing her core against his body. As she pushed her chest against his, the stiff peaks of her nipples rubbed against the sports bra, creating tantalizing friction against the fabric.

He growled into her mouth, the sound vibrating inside her, and she sighed her pleasure into his mouth.

Varg walked her backward until her back hit the door. He placed his hands on the wood so that they bracketed her head and pushed himself away from her. "If you don't want this, tell me now," he said, resting his forehead against hers, his chest heaving. He grabbed the door handle by her hip. "Once I open this door, and we step inside, I'm not going to be able to stop." Leaning back, he looked into her eyes, searching for an answer.

She stared back. His irises were lighter but not quite the color of his wolf's. Caressing his neck with her fingertips, she tried to think logically. She wanted him so bad, but technically he was a client now.

He kissed her temple and trailed his lips down to her ear. "Stop touching me, or I'm going to lose control." His hot breath caressed her neck, and she couldn't help but close her eyes and tilt her head to give him better access. "Marconi," he growled in warning.

A rough giggled escaped her lips. "I think we should start using first names."

"Elaine," he said, pulled down the collar of her t-shirt with his teeth and nipped her collar bone.

Heat flooded between her legs. "Laney," she sighed. "Nobody calls me Elaine."

"Make up your mind, Laney." He nuzzled her neck and then nipped her earlobe.

Her nipples were about to bust through the sports bra.

She couldn't sleep with a client. *Yes, you can*, her hormones shouted.

Screw it. She wanted him. And they hadn't signed a contract yet. Technically he wasn't a client.

Rising up on her tiptoes, she buried her fingers in his short hair.

She molded herself to his body and claimed his mouth with hers.

His tongue met hers thrust for thrust, and he grabbed her hip with the hand not on the door handle. "Are you saying yes," he asked. "I need to hear it."

"Yes," she breathed into his mouth.

He groaned and swept his hand down her thigh. Hooking the back of her knee, he lifted her leg over his hip and pressed his hardness straight into her core. Her panties dampened, and her breath quickened. "Open the damn door," she groaned."

He chuckled and twisted the handle. As the door swung

open, he pushed her through, turning her so that her back pressed against his chest. As the door closed with a snick, he slid her panties and pants down her hips. She stepped out of her shoes, socks, and clothes all at the same time.

He gripped her hips, pressing the bulge on the front of his jeans into the cleft between her bare buttocks. Her skin heated under his hands, and she arched her back.

The tips of his fingers touched her damp pubic curls, and he slid his right hand lower so he could bury a finger inside her. With the heel of his hand, he pressed against her mound.

White heat flickered on the inside of her eyelids as her core clenched around his finger.

His teeth scraped the skin on her neck, and then he bit her shoulder as a second finger joined the first.

Laney panted hard, trying to catch her breath as her heart beat so fast, it might jump out of her chest. "Varg," she moaned, gripping his wrist.

"Arek," he corrected. "We're on a first-name basis now, remember." His fingers curled inside her wet core, and he squeezed.

She whimpered, pressing her butt back against him.

With a growl, he slipped his fingers out of her and grabbed the hem of her t-shirt.

She helped him pull it over her head and then grabbed the sports bra, which followed the shirt to land somewhere on the floor.

Arek paused for a moment and stared at her bare breasts. He grabbed her hand, pulled her toward him, and lifted her into his arms. A few steps later, she sailed through the air as he hoisted her onto the bed. With one hand, he grabbed the back of his shirt collar and pulled the garment over his head.

Laney bit her lip as she stared at his sculptured chest and abs. The Odin medallion rested against the fine blond hair that dusted his pectorals and then narrowed to a darker strip that disappeared into his jeans. "Pants too," she breathed out as she locked gazes with him.

His pupils dilated, and a smile filled with male satisfaction played on his lips. "As you command." He unzipped the jeans and pulled them down with the boxer briefs underneath. As his erection sprung free, he hissed and stepped out of his shoes and socks.

Laney scooted backward on the bed to make room for him, but he caught her ankle and stopped her. "Not so fast," he growled. "I want a taste." Her brows furrowed as she tried to make sense of his words, but a fraction of a second later, she had her answer as he kneeled beside the bed. He dragged her closer so that her butt was right on the edge of the mattress.

Draping her legs over his shoulders, he lowered his face to her core. As his tongue pressed against her clit, she cried out. A shock of white-hot pleasure shot from her center and spread through her body. She couldn't catch her breath and moaned Arek's name as she buried her hands in his hair, pressing herself against his mouth.

He pushed his hands under her butt, tilting her pelvis to give himself better access. His teeth scraped her clit, and he sucked her hard as he pushed a thumb inside her.

Laney shattered. Wave after wave of heat shook her body, the pleasure so intense, her hips shot off the mattress.

Arek gripped her buttocks hard and kept nipping and sucking clit, swallowing her juices down as her climax pulsed for several moments.

When the swell had peaked, and the aftershocks settled down, his mouth finally released her.

Laney tried to say something, but her breath came in such short bursts she couldn't form any words. She wasn't sure what she'd say anyway. Thanks for the best orgasm, ever? She giggled.

Arek wiped his chin with the back of his hand and smiled as he looked down at her. "I amuse you?"

"You amaze me," she breathed out, her body limp and sweaty against the bed cover. She pushed herself up on her elbows. "Let me return the favor."

He shook his head. "We're not done yet." Hooking one arm underneath her knees and draping the other around her shoulders, he climbed onto the bed with her in his arms. Half sitting down with his shoulders against the headboard, he positioned Laney on his lap and leaned down to kiss her deeply. "Ready for round two?" he said when she was once again panting and looking at him in a glazed-over stupor.

Her nipples ached for his touch, and she grabbed his hand and pressed her breast into his palm.

His pupils widened, and he kneaded her flesh, hard.

She twisted and straddled him. Leaning down to claim his lips with hers, she sucked his tongue into her mouth.

As she lowered her hips and took him inside her, Arek groaned loudly, releasing her breast to grip her hips.

She lifted herself and then sunk down again, taking all of his length this time.

The tip of his cock bumped against her cervix, causing just enough pain to give her pleasure the edge she wanted.

He tilted his hands so his fingers dug into the flesh of her buttocks. His tongue laved one of her nipples, and then his teeth nipped the sensitive peak before he sucked the whole areola into his mouth. Arek kept sucking and biting, driving her mad with desire.

Laney rode him faster, her hands on his shoulders for balance.

He squeezed her hips and buttocks harder, pushing hard each downstroke so he could bury himself deeper inside her.

His mouth released the one nipple and captured the other.

As he bit down on the hardened peak, Laney exploded.

Her back arched, and she ground herself down so hard against him, she could feel his hip bones digging into the inside of her thighs. Her legs pressed against his, and her breath came in short bursts.

Arek released her hips, pushed her breasts together between his palms, captured both nipples with his mouth, and then gently bit down.

Another wave of climax shuddered through Laney's body.

As she cried out, he gripped her hips again and pumped inside her hard and quick.

She felt him erupt inside her, and as he found his release, he roared her name.

Laney collapsed, every muscle in her body limp. She leaned against him, waiting for her breath to slow down.

Arek pushed back her hair and bracketed her face with his palms so he could look at her. "Are you okay?" His eyes were deep blue again.

She nodded. "Very okay."

He scooted them both down and gently rolled her off him. Lying face-to-face, he played with her hair, tucking it behind her ear. "We didn't use protection," he said. "But humans can't catch diseases from shifters, and wolves can only impregnate their true mates."

"What does that mean?" she asked.

"True mates?"

She grinned. "Yes, I already know what impregnate means."

He chuckled, tracing a finger down the side of her face. It seemed Arek Varg liked tactile contact. She didn't mind. She was a cuddler herself. "When shifters meet their true mate, their animal side claim them for life."

She raised herself on one elbow. "But you live for a very

long time." Witches aged slower than regular humans, but shifters could live for centuries. "How old are you anyway."

He interlaced his fingers with hers and tugged, so she fell against his chest. Pulling a blanket over them both, he said, "It's not polite asking a wolf his age, but for your information, I became a wolf in the early 1900s, when I was in my early thirties."

Dang. She'd just had sex with grandpa wolf. Not that she minded, he'd obviously picked up a trick or two to use in bed during the last century. She smiled against his skin.

"What are you laughing about," he asked.

"Nothing," she said. "Just thinking about our age difference." She raised her chin so she could see his face. "I'm twenty-eight. You're robbing the cradle."

He smiled down at her. "Do you mind?"

"Not at all." She traced her finger around his nipple and watched it pucker. "I may have some questions for you, though, about history."

He captured her hand and brought it to his lips. "Of course, you do." He kissed her finger one by one and then sucked her thumb into his mouth.

Her core clenched, and her nipples tingled. "Round three?" she said half-jokingly.

He released her thumb, a wicked grin stretching his lips. "I thought you'd never ask." Apparently, being alive for more than a century had not tempered his stamina.

She was a very fortunate girl.

CHAPTER 12

$\mathscr{A}$rek startled awake, trying to figure out where he was. The warm body draped over his chest helped him retrieve his memory. Dr. Marconi—Laney—grunted in her sleep like a little cub. Someone knocked softly on the door to the suite, again. That was the sound that had woken him.

He untangled himself gently from the sleeping witch and slid out of bed. Soundlessly, he padded on bare feet across the suite's sitting room to the door on the other side.

"Yeah," he said in a low voice. Outside the window, pale tendrils of morning sun streaked the sky.

"It's Bolt. Sorry to wake you. But you need to see this."

"Give me a second." His second in command wouldn't have bothered him unless it was urgent. Arek pulled on his clothes and pulled the comforter over Laney before leaving the bedroom.

She mumbled something in her sleep, but he couldn't make out the words.

He joined his lieutenant in the hallway.

Bolt looked him over. "Was that wise? She's a witch." Unhappiness and anger traveled down the pack bond. What the fuck was this about?

"Not interested in your opinion," Arek shot back. "Why are you here." He frowned. Justice, Bolt, and he were tight, but they didn't discuss each other's choice of bed partners. What did Bolt have against Laney? Arek had slept with witches before.

His lieutenant pushed his hands deep into his pockets. "Someone just called Justice about two dead wolves. They washed ashore on Kirby Cove Beach."

Fuck. "Drowning? Who are they?"

"I don't have many details. We drove down to confirm that they were indeed wolves. Once we figured that out, I came back here to get you."

"Who called?" If someone knew the body belonged to wolves, it was most likely another shifter.

"The campground attendant is part of a local mountain lion clan. He recognized the bodies as shifters." Bolt rocked on his heels. "The campground has a few overnight guests. The lion wants us to get the bodies out of there as soon as possible."

Right. If regular humans got involved, it would get a lot messier. Their law enforcement usually stayed out of shifter business, but dead bodies at a public campground would be hard to keep out of the press. "Let's go," Arek said, heading down the stairs to the first floor.

"I can meet up with Justice again and bring the bodies here," Bolt offered. "You should shower before we go. I can smell her on you." His nose wrinkled in distaste.

Arek stopped, took a moment to collect himself, and then stepped into his lieutenant's personal space. "What is your problem?"

Bolt started back. It took a strong wolf to meet an alpha's stare. Both of his lieutenants were dominant enough to lead packs of their own, but so far, they'd never expressed an interest.

Leading alpha wolves was a delicate balancing act. Arek dealt with it by encouraging them to express their opinions, but Bolt's behavior tonight bordered on disrespectful. Arek's wolf growled his displeasure.

His lieutenant dropped his gaze. "No problem," he said. "None of my business."

"Let's keep it that way," Arek shot over his shoulder as they descended the rest of the stairs. With Novikov's wife and her brother in his territory, he did not have time for a mutiny. Especially not in his own house.

* * *

As THE CROW FLEW, it was only a few thousand feet from the Pack House to Kirby Cove Beach, but the Marin Headlands consisted mainly of rock formations and hills. Since they needed a car to transport the bodies in, they had to follow the serpentine roads for almost half an hour before they met up with Justice. If they'd run as wolves, they'd been there in only a few minutes.

The beach lay just below an old maritime artillery battery that hadn't been in service since the early 1930s. Because of the military building, a drivable road led all the way down to the beach from the headlands. They parked the van by the battery and crossed the sand to where Justice stood next to a Caucasian man with sandy blond hair.

The man, who smelled like a mountain lion shifter, introduced himself as Peter Cavalier, the campground attendant. "Luckily, none of the campers are up yet," he said. "This bunch seems less interested in hiking or surfing. They spend most of their time hanging around their tents, drinking beer. They're not early risers, but that doesn't mean one of them won't wander down here at some point."

Arek shook his hand. "Thanks for calling us." He looked toward the surf's edge where two bodies lay and then met Justice's eyes. His enforcer moved his head a fraction of a millimeter—a minuscule head shake. For some reason, Justice didn't want him to ask the obvious question about who the two wolves were.

Cavalier looked up the hill to the campsite's location. "I'll head back up. If any of the campers are awake, I'll stall them." He crossed the sand and started on the walking trail that led to the campground, but Arek still didn't ask Justice who the two wolves were. Mountain lions had excellent hearing. Instead, he crouched down by the bodies.

They'd been in the water for more than a day. The fish had already nibbled on them. However, despite missing the tip of their noses and most of their eyes, he recognized them right away. They were the two men that had wrecked Laney's apartment. Novikov's wolves. That's why Justice hadn't wanted to discuss their identity.

Fuck. Two dead rival wolves, just down the road from his Pack House. This could turn ugly. The last thing they needed was for other shifter clans to get involved in wolf politics.

He stood.

Both Bolt and Justice looked at him with grim faces that probably echoed his expression. "There's a reason they were dumped so close to the Pack House," Bolt said. He must also have recognized the bodies.

"It's a message," Justice echoed.

"Yeah, but what does it mean?" Arek wanted to know.

"Doesn't have to have any deeper meaning than Novikov fucking with us," Bolt said.

Arek nodded. "I'm sick of that alpha messing around in my territory."

"This trouble all started with the witch," Bolt said bitterly.

Justice did a double-take. He patted Bolt's shoulder. "You alright, Mate?" He frowned. "The witch stole the medallion, but Novikov set her up. She's not the cause of this problem. She's Novikov's target. Same as us."

Bolt shrugged. "I'll back the van up," he said, walking back up the beach to the road.

"What the fuck is his problem?" Justice asked.

"I have no idea," Arek said. "Let's load the bodies and get out of here before the humans wake up."

Justice walked on the other side of him and suddenly stopped. He grinned. "I'm downwind from you now," he said. "I think I know what Bolt's problem is. You slept with Dr. Marconi."

Arek frowned. "I've slept with witches before, and Bolt's never had a problem." Did his lieutenant have feelings for Laney? Was that what this was all about.

Arek's wolf stirred. It didn't like anyone but them close to the sexy witch.

He hadn't noticed Bolt showing particular interest. Intense emotions, like desire, were hard to block from other wolves. As alpha, Arek especially would have picked up on Bolt's feelings through the pack bond.

"You usually don't bring your conquests to the Pack House," Justice said as he lifted one of the bodies in a fireman carry. His nose wrinkled. "This fellow stinks." As he headed up the beach, he grinned over his shoulder at Arek. "I think our little brother is jealous because Daddy has a new girlfriend."

Arek grabbed the other dead wolf, hoisted him over his shoulder, and followed his enforcer up the beach. "She's not my girlfriend. And I'm sure I've brought women to the Pack

House before." But had he? He hadn't had a serious relationship in decades. He couldn't remember if he'd ever brought a dates home.

"Not to spend the night," Justice threw over his shoulder. "You prefer to sleep at their house so you can sneak out in the morning or leave if things get too emotionally complex." They'd reached the car, and he loaded the body into the back of the van, which Bolt had opened. Wiping his hands on his pants, he grinned at Arek. "I use the same trick, Mate."

"What are you two chatting about?" Bolt asked.

"Nothing," Arek said as he dumped the body next to the other dead wolf. They did smell bad. The rot and decay lingered in the air. A lot of bleach would be required to clean the van properly.

But Justice patted Bolt's shoulder. "We're discussing how to help you deal with your alpha having a girlfriend."

Bolt just grunted and went to open the driver's door.

"Not my girlfriend," Arek insisted, feeling ill at ease now. He must have brought home a date to the Pack House at some point. Just because he couldn't remember it didn't mean it didn't happen.

"Keep telling yourself that, Mate," Justice said as he opened the sliding door and jumped into the back seat.

Arek slid into the passenger front seat, next to Bolt.

Maybe he needed to make sure Laney didn't have any expectations beyond casual sex. Their time together had been spectacular.

Correction, explosive.

He definitely wanted a repeat experience, but he did not need a girlfriend. Emotions complicated things—made them messy. He had enough messes on his hands trying to lead the Coalition, even when Novikov's wife was not running amok in his territory.

There was no room for additional complications in his life. And girlfriends definitely made things complicated.

His wolf growled. *Not girlfriend. Mate.*

Great, now the beast was obsessed with Laney. As if his life wasn't enough of a hot mess already.

CHAPTER 13

*L*aney left the shielded room in the basement and climbed the stairs to the first floor, where she headed straight to the kitchen. She'd spent the morning organizing Varg's—Arek's—collection. As she'd requested, the room now had a top-of-the-line laptop resting on an adjustable glass and chrome desk. In the room, she'd also found several large sacks of salt and a water-filled aquarium big enough to house a shark.

If she came across an item infused with dark magic or ancient magic that had grown out of control, which the Witch and Mage Council had named wild magic, she'd hopefully be able to null its effects inside a warded salt circle.

As a last resort, she'd dump it into the tank of saltwater. The problem with that was she'd damage the artifact, and a priceless historical record could be lost forever.

Speaking of lost things, she hadn't been able to track down the alpha of the house all day.

She'd woken up alone, which was a bit of a disappointment, but also a relief since mornings after could be awkward. She blushed, thinking about how she'd fallen asleep after Arek had given her a fourth orgasm.

He might be an old wolf, but he'd certainly learned new tricks—unless people were way more sexually advanced at the beginning of the twentieth century. Her stomach growled, and she shook her head to stop thinking about sex and concentrate on a different kind of hunger.

Bolt had shown her the kitchen briefly during their tour, but she'd forgotten its vast size. The chef who cooked the evening meals didn't arrive until the afternoon. Bolt had told her everyone in the house foraged for lunch on their own, but the chef often left them sandwiches or meat platters in the fridge. He'd told her to help herself. The words had been polite, but his tone gruff.

She had no idea what he had against her. Hopefully, it was just his prejudice against witches and not anything personal.

She placed the notebook she'd brought with her on the counter and opened one of the industrial-sized refrigerators, hoping today's lunch treat would involve sandwiches.

As much as she liked meat, a whole meal of just protein was a little too much. Her wishes were heard, and she found a plate of turkey and Swiss on rye, her favorite. She tore off a sheet of paper towel from the dispenser on the counter and grabbed one of the sandwiches. After only three tries, she found the cabinet that held glasses and filled one with tap water. She then brought all her food and the notebook through a pair of double doors to the dining room.

Eating in the sunroom would be fabulous, but she wanted to get some work done, and that would not happen with the spectacular view on display.

As she munched on her sandwich, she opened up her notebook and grabbed her pen. She'd hoped to be able to start cataloging the artifact collection right away, but it was in such disarray that she didn't even know where to start.

The items were shelved, but not in any particular order or according to any kind of system.

For a few minutes, she'd contemplating just putting them all in a big pile in the middle of the room so she'd have empty shelves with which to start.

She'd found the ledgers that Arek had talked about, but they didn't seem to follow any order either. They were mostly a bunch of scribbles that supposedly described an item, but most of the wordings were so vague, they could refer to several articles. One of the entries had simply been, "knife."

Considering she'd so far counted more than a hundred blades, daggers, and sickles, the entry was less than helpful.

There had even been a few scalpels. She shuddered.

Historical medical tools were not for the faint of heart. And if they were infused with magic, they were even worse. The difference between torture and ancient surgical procedures was very fine.

Laney scribbled in her notebook, trying to come up with broad main categories to sort the collection. Should she go by origin? Purpose? Maybe the strength of their power? She'd have to ask Arek what system made the most sense to him.

Thinking about the wolf made certain parts of her body tingle. Parts that were a little sore, but she didn't mind. She should have an ethical problem about sleeping with someone she worked for. However, after last night, she'd find a way to get her principles to stand down because there was no way she was passing up having sex with Arek again. There could, of course, never be anything more serious between them. She didn't do relationships.

She'd had a few casual boyfriends and one very serious one. A fellow academic, he'd dumped her as soon as her graduate student had accused her of sexual harassment.

Falsely accused her, but her lover hadn't even considered her side of the story. She shook her head. That was in the past and not something she'd dwell on now. It had taught her a valuable lesson. She should be grateful for that.

As long as she and Arek enjoyed exploring each other's bodies, they could continue sleeping together. Eventually, one of them would get bored, or she'd be done with the catalog project. She paused in her scribbles, more likely the former.

The double doors from the kitchen flew open, and Nora entered. "Hey," she said, striding up to the table. "Just the person I'm looking for."

"Here I am," Laney said, stretching out her arms.

The lawyer smiled and sat down on the opposite side of the table. "You said the Witch and Mage Council spend a lot of resources keeping Inessa from acquiring magical artifacts?"

Laney nodded. "I don't know the details, but she's on the council's blacklist. Theoretically, auction houses and artifact brokers are not supposed to sell to people on the list."

"Okay," Nora tapped on the tablet she'd brought. "I have this idea about why Inessa and her brother are here, other than to fuck with the pack, of course." She turned the screen toward Laney. "There's a big benefit dinner ending in an artifact auction in Sarasota later this week."

Laney looked down at the tablet. A newspaper article described a children's charity benefit, ending with a paddle auction of historical items donated by private collectors. It didn't say specifically that the artifacts were of the magical kind, but reading the list of donors, it seemed very likely. "This is the kind of auction at which someone like Inessa might be able to nab a few items," she told Nora. "If I was a black-listed dark witch, this is where I would shop."

Nora grinned big. "Excellent. Then all I have to do is get an invite."

"Why not just tell the Witch and Mage Council that the siblings are likely to be at the auction?"

The lawyer tilted her head. "And what will they do other than try to stop them from buying artifacts? Inessa and Iakov broke pack laws. They must be dealt with, or Arek loses respect as alpha. Besides, this is a shifter matter, not a council matter."

"Okay, then what will you do once you get to the benefit? Can shifters counteract dark magic?" She wasn't facetious. She wanted to know if the wolves had a secret weapon against dark magic."

"I'm not going," Nora said. "The invitation will be for you and Arek, with Justice and Bolt as backup."

Laney blinked. "Come again." No way she'd attend the benefit. It would be crawling with her former colleagues. Her ex would probably be there too.

The lawyer stood. "I've already cleared it with the alpha and have arranged for a dress and accessories for you." She powered down the tablet screen and tucked the device under her arm. "We don't want people to know about the collection in the basement, so Arek will pretend to be your boyfriend, and you'll pretend to represent a wealthy collector who wishes to remain anonymous."

"Do I have a say in this?" Laney asked, her voice wobbling a little. "Shouldn't you clear this with me?" She may be working for...consulting for the pack alpha, but she hadn't signed up for confronting a dark witch and her dark mage brother. Because they were siblings, they probably enhanced each other's magic. And if Iakov actually was the man who'd flogged her in the storage facility, she did not want to meet him again.

"I'm sorry," Nora sank back down into the chair. "That

was insensitive of me. Of course, you have a say in this. Talk it over with Arek."

"Where is your alpha?" Laney asked.

"The two wolves who ransacked your apartment were found dead this morning, washed ashore not too far from here. Arek, together with Justice and Bolt, is trying to figure out what killed them."

"Not drowning then?"

Nora shook her head. "There's no water in their lungs and not a mark on their bodies."

Great, two dead bodies, killed under mysterious circumstances. That didn't sound like a dark ritual at all. "Poison?"

The lawyer studied her for a beat. "Would you be able to tell what killed them if it was through magic?"

Laney studied her hands. Probably. But that didn't mean she wanted to examine the bodies. She swallowed. "Most likely."

Nora stood again. "Please come with me."

Dark magic left a foul stain on its victims long after the sacrificial ceremony. Non-practitioners were usually not affected, but anyone else who wielded powers had to be careful. This consulting gig was already way more complicated than Laney had expected.

She had many clauses to add to the contract that she still hadn't seen or signed.

CHAPTER 14

They'd started with the bodies in the shed in the backyard, but they stank so horribly Justice insisted they'd drag the folding tables outside and examine the dead wolves there.

"Is it my imagination, or are they decomposing faster than normal?" Arek asked. "Or, is it just the smell that's getting worse?"

Justice held an arm in front of his face. "I don't know, Mate, but they're definitely more rank than they were thirty minutes ago. Aren't you supposed to get used to bad smells after a while?"

"When will the doctor get here?" Bolt asked. Although not technically a medical examiner, the pack doctor had performed autopsies before.

"She's not," Justice answered. "She's out of town for the next few days at some medical conference."

Arek sighed. They'd opened up one of the wolves to examine the lungs. They were dry. Assuming the two assholes had died the same way, neither of them had drowned. Their next step had been the worst, investigating the body's surfaces for blunt trauma or weapon marks. The smell had been horrible, especially to their sensitive noses. They hadn't found any clues of what killed the wolves. "I'm going to have to call the other alphas and let them know about this."

Bolt shook his head. "Don't. Let's go over them one more time. If you call the alphas without knowing what happened, they'll just speculate and create drama. None of it will be helpful, and it will suck up all of our time."

He wasn't wrong. But what other option did they have?

His wolf perked up. *Mate.*

He did not need his beast fixated on Laney, confusing great sex with a true mate bonding. As if he didn't have enough to deal with. And why was the dumb animal perking up now? He rubbed his chest, telling the beast mentally to stand down.

Ours, Wolf growled.

Justice shot him an amused look before focusing on someone over Arek's shoulder. "Hey," the enforcer said. "Welcome to the palace of horrible smells."

Arek turned around to find Laney and Nora walking toward them. His beast perked up even more.

The lawyer carried a big sack of something on her shoulder. "I've brought the witch who's currently staying with us. Maybe she knows something about what may have killed the wolves who worked for the dark witch and her mage brother." Sarcasm practically dripped from each of Nora's words.

"Great idea," Justice said. "What else did you bring us, Santa?" He pointed at the sack on Nora's shoulder.

The lawyer dropped her load on the ground. "Salt, you barmy Brit."

Justice laughed and walked up to Laney. "I hope you can

figure out what the hell killed these gits. We have no clue." He put his hands on her shoulder.

Arek's wolf made him growl out loud. Mine.

The three pack members stared at him. His wolf focused on Justice. *Mine*, it repeated.

The Brit grinned wide and lifted both hands, palms forward. He slowly stepped away from the witch. "Easy there, Mate. Everything's fine."

Laney's head swiveled back and forth between Justice and Arek. "What's going on."

"Just male wolves having some testosterone overload problems," Nora said with a grin just as wide as Justice's. "They'll calm down in a minute."

Laney gave him a shy smile. "Hi."

Mate, his wolf repeated, almost purring. Arek cursed inwardly. He'd hoped he was wrong about his wolf claiming Laney, but the dumb beast thought she was their mate. Who'd ever heard of a witch being a shifter's true mate? Ridiculous.

Plus, the mating bond was something the beast and the human sides decided on together. The wolf was just obsessed with Laney because it had been a while since Arek had a bed partner.

Some of his thoughts must have displayed on his face because Laney quickly turned away from him, but not before he saw hurt flashing in her eyes.

He didn't want her as his mate, but that didn't mean he wanted to cause her pain. He took a step toward her, but she ignored him.

"Right," she said to Nora. "We need a separate salt circle around each body. If they're warded or cursed, they may interfere with or feed power to each other."

The lawyer hoisted the sack of salt, tore a small hole in one of the corners, and walked around each of the bodies until a consistent stream of white granules encapsulated each table.

As she closed the last circle, Bolt exhaled loudly.

The smell from the dead wolves decreased in intensity.

"Why didn't we think of that," Justice asked.

Laney slowly walked around the body nearest her, the wolf whose lung they hadn't sliced open. She leaned closer, scrutinizing the ear. "What did you do with their clothes?"

"Burned them," Bolt said. "They stank."

"Did you go through their pockets first?"

"Of course," Arek said. "There was nothing inside any of them."

Laney nodded. "Empty pockets. Empty head," she mumbled.

"What does that mean," Justice asked.

Nora shushed him. "Let her work."

Laney walked over to the almost empty sack of salt that Nora had deposited on the ground. She reached in and rubbed her hands in the granules. "I don't know very much about dark magic," she said to Nora. "But I think these bodies have been cursed with an ancient spell."

"Do you know what killed them?" Arek asked her. He rubbed his chest again. The damn wolf kept prancing, wanting to touch Laney.

She shrugged. "Maybe. It's a long shot, but it's all I got."

"Go for it," Nora urged.

Laney took her shoes off and flexed her toes in the grass. She looked at Justice. "It might work better if you all take a few steps back."

It pissed Arek off that she spoke to his second-in-command instead of him. His wolf hissed. Actually hissed, like a damn cat.

Nora and Justice exchanged a look, both grinning like idiots. Glad he could entertain them.

Bolt just shook his head and stepped back from the tables, but his face had lost some of the tension that had been there since the morning.

Arek joined his pack members a few paces away from the witch and the bodies. He knew his eyes flashed ice-blue because the damn wolf wouldn't stand down, but there was nothing he could do about it.

Laney widened her stance and closed her eyes. She twisted her head from side to side and rotated her shoulders. Inhaling deeply, she raised her hands hip-level with her palms facing the sky. Another breath, and she lifted them to shoulder level. A slight breeze ruffled her hair, and she tilted her head back, her face up toward the sky.

The slight air current strengthened into a gusty wind, whipping her hair around her face. None of it reached Arek or the wolves.

She stretched her hands higher and rotated them, so her palms faced each other above her head. The wind died down, but the ground under her feet rippled. She opened her eyes and lowered her arms, hugging herself. Walking backward just outside the salt line, she circumscribed first one table and then the other.

Arek could see her lips moving, but he couldn't hear her words.

She moved her hands, cupping her shoulders, her arms crossed in front of her chest. Still walking backward, she followed a figure-eight path, weaving around the tables. She stopped, and two loud pops sounded, like small firecrackers.

Laney sunk to the ground. He ran toward her. "I'm okay," she said as he reached her. "Just really tired. Did it work?" She pushed off the ground to stand, and Arek cupped her elbow, helping her rise. When she swayed, he put his arm around her shoulders.

"I think it did," Justice said. "If by 'working' you mean shrink these fellow's skulls."

Arek turned to look at the dead wolves. Their heads looked like large raisins.

"What happened to them," Nora asked.

Laney pushed against Arek, but he kept his hand around her as she walked closer to the tables. "Empty pockets. Empty Minds," she said again. "It's this weird rhyme little kids with magical abilities learn. I found an old stone slab a few years ago that had those words inscribed on it, but they were part of a dark magic curse."

"What does the curse do?" Bolt asked.

Laney hesitated and scrunched up her nose. "It took me a while to find that out, but I discovered an old manuscript that had the same spell and also described the outcome. Basically, it turns your brain and skull into sludge that leaks out your ears."

Nora gagged.

"Are you saying Inessa or Iakov completely lobotomized these men?" Arek asked, cold anger growing in the pit of his stomach. These weren't his pack members, and he probably would've killed them himself once he caught them. But he'd made it an honorable death. An honorable fight. This was a pathetic and cruel way to die.

"Fucking zombies," Justice mumbled.

Bolt stared at the two bodies on the table, a glistening sheen covering his face. He turned and almost ran into the house.

Arek was glad he'd skipped lunch. The stench of the bodies had made him lose his appetite. He squeezed Laney's shoulders. "Are you okay," he asked.

She nodded. "I just need to lie down for a while. This required more energy than I thought." She walked over to retrieve her shoes and then continued into the house without looking at him.

Arek sighed. He had to talk to her later, but he had an unpleasant video conference to organize for now. He could only imagine how up in arms the coalition's alphas would be when he told him about dark magic turning wolf heads into dried husks.

CHAPTER 15

wo days later, Laney walked down the stairs, holding the hem of the exquisite aqua-colored dress Nora had bought for her. Her feet were strapped into a pair of stiletto silver sandals, and she carried a matching clutch. The shoes' straps went above the ankle, which made them more comfortable to walk in, but she'd still need to watch what she drank tonight.

The three-inch heels would make it hard not to tumble even while sober. Hopefully, Inessa and Iakov would behave civilized if they showed up tonight. If Laney had to run to get away from them, she'd be toast unless she ditched the shoes, of course. It would be a shame, though. They were so pretty.

She reached the landing, and when she turned to take the final steps down to the entryway, she looked up to see Arek waiting for her at the bottom of the stairs.

Laney had to stop and take a deep breath. Arek Varg in a tailored tuxedo was a sight to behold. The coat's black starkness and the shirt's white crispness should have washed out his light skin and blond hair. Instead, they highlighted his face's sharp planes and gave the perfect canvas for his azure blue eyes to look even more intense. She told her hormones to stand down and continued down the steps.

She hadn't seen him since the afternoon they determined what killed the two wolves. He'd traveled for the last few days to visit with other pack leaders and take care of some business stuff. He hadn't told her the details.

She'd missed him, which annoyed her. The collection had kept her busy during the days, but her nights had been filled with dreams of the alpha.

Arek moved toward her, holding out a hand to support her. "Wow, you look amazing." Male appreciation shone in his eyes, which never left hers, despite the generous cleavage the dress put on display.

She took his hand and tried not to react to the heat that sizzled between them as their skin touched. "Thank you. Nora has the perfect eye for my size and what color would suit me."

He chuckled. "She didn't pick out the dress. Justice did."

Okay, so that was a little creepy. She didn't know the Brit had spent that much time cataloging her body. "I'll have to thank him," she said with an awkward smile, letting go of Arek's hand.

Arek must have picked up on her discomfort. "He takes one look at a person and instantly knows what would suit them. It's like a low-grade super power he has." He gestured toward his outfit. "He picked this for me. I didn't even have to visit the tailor. It fit perfectly with what Justice gave them to work with."

Okay, that made her feel a little bit better. She allowed herself one more perusal of the splendid form of Arek in the tux. "Well, he certainly picked out what would make you look good."

"Ah, so you're saying I'm good-looking tonight." His eyes twinkled.

Oh, please. The man knew he was devastatingly handsome. "You clean up well," she said. He didn't need her to fan his ego.

"Shall we?" Arek gestured toward the door.

She nodded, and they walked out together, him holding the door open for her. Outside, a black limousine waited for them, and he helped her into the back seat. The soft leather hugged her body.

Arek slid into the backseat from the other door. He turned to the driver. "Hey, it's your job to open and close doors."

Bolt turned to grin at them from the front seat. "Got it, Boss."

Laney did a double-take. She'd never seen Bolt smile, and she'd never seen him dressed in anything but jeans or sweats. Tonight, he wore a dark suit, looking every bit like a driver who doubles as a bodyguard. He'd been in a much better mood ever since they figured out what killed the east-coast wolves.

She'd known Bolt would be their driver and that Justice would follow behind on a motorcycle, but she hadn't expected the limo.

"You went all out," she said to Arek as the car rolled down the driveway.

"What kind of boyfriend would I be if I didn't spend my money to impress my date?" He lifted her hand and brushed his lips across it, barely touching her skin. His eyes never left hers, and when she shivered, a smile of male satisfaction graced his mouth.

The heat sizzling through her body from where his lips had touched her hand combined with her nerves became sensation overload, and she quickly pulled her hand away.

Arek frowned. "Did I do something wrong?"

"Just nervous," she said. "I'm not good at pretending. Plus, there is going to be some people there that I haven't seen in a long time." She hadn't stayed in touch with any of her former colleagues from the university. Not that they'd reached out to her once the false accusations had forced her to resign. And if her ex showed up, which seemed likely since he managed the university's artifacts acquisitions department, she wasn't sure she could play her role.

Seeing him tonight, on top of pretending to date Arek, on top of hunting down Inessa, the dark witch, was a little much to deal with.

"Don't be," Arek said. "I will be by your side the whole night, and Bolt will be there to protect you too."

Their driver met her gaze in the rearview mirror. "Got that right," he said with another grin. She finally figured out why he was so happy. Bolt was looking forward to a fight.

"It's not that," Laney said. "I didn't leave the university on good terms, and some of my colleagues will be there tonight."

"That's what happens when you get caught sleeping with your students," Bolt chimed in. "You should have been more careful."

She bristled and straightened in her seat. "So, you're saying the sleeping part was okay, but I was stupid getting caught?"

Bolt nodded.

She looked at Arek. "What do you think?" His answer mattered more than it should, and it irritated her.

He held up his hands, palm facing her. "I don't know the particulars, and so I have no opinion. Maybe you were in love with this guy, and the two of you couldn't wait until he was no longer in your class."

Laney shook her head. At least he kept an open mind, but she hated having this stupid scandal that wasn't even true hanging over her head. "I didn't sleep with my student. It would be unethical and unprofessional. Also, he wasn't in my class. I was his thesis advisor." She sighed. "He thought he deserved to graduate early, and when I disagreed, he accused me of making sexual advances. He told my department chair and dean that I wouldn't sign off on his thesis because he had turned me down."

"But if it wasn't true, that shouldn't have mattered," Arek said. "Once they investigated, they would have figured out that he wasn't ready to graduate, and so there was probably nothing to his accusations."

Laney smiled wryly. "The university had recently made a big deal about passing a policy about sexual harassment that included to start any investigation from the position of believing the victim." She brushed an invisible speck of lint off her knee. "The irony is that I was the chair of the committee who pushed through the change of policy."

Arek took your hand. "I bet you pissed off some people doing that. Not everyone responds well to change."

She nodded, taking comfort in how good her hand felt in his. "I did indeed. One of them was my department chair, with who I'd had other disagreements as well." Her supervisor's betrayal still felt raw, even though it had been two years since the incident now. "He decided that my student's project *was* ready and that it meant his accusations had merits. As so often happens in these cases, the sexual harassment charges came down to my word against my student's, and in the end, nothing was proven."

"So why did you leave," Arek asked.

"Because there was a stain on my reputation, which meant that most opportunities were now closed to me." She didn't add the derision and disbelief she'd received from former colleagues whom she thought were friends or that the classes she was offered to teach from then on were the ones nobody else wanted. Or that her research project's budget all of a sudden got cut.

But worst of all was James's betrayal. They'd talked about marriage. That's how in love she'd thought herself, how much she thought he loved her. He'd dumped her the same night she found out her student would graduate after all.

Arek caressed her hand. "Well, tonight, you return triumphantly with a billionaire boyfriend at your side, representing a reclusive collector who trusts only your opinion about what to buy."

She smiled. Wouldn't that be wonderful? Not the boyfriend part. She was done with those and preferred to support herself, but rubbing her colleagues—and James's—noses in how she now had access to a much more impressive collection of artifacts than what the university owned would be fantastic.

In a way, it wasn't so far from the truth. She did represent Arek, even if they still hadn't signed a contract. And he did have an extensive and impressive collection, even if it would take decades to sort out precisely what he'd acquired.

"What exactly were your plans for the items in the basement?"

He shrugged. "I didn't have a plan. I just acquired items that somebody could use against shifters and dumped them in the basement. Someone told me I should shield the room with lead, so I did."

"Where did you find the money to do all that?"

He raised her hand and nibbled on her fingertip. "Did you miss the part where I told you I'm a billionaire?"

"You were serious?" She knew he was wealthy, but a billionaire?

Arek laughed. "It's amazing what you can do on the stock market when your long-game can last a century. Plus, the security company is doing well."

"What do you spend your money on?"

"The stuff in the basement." He smiled. "Seriously, most of

the money is tied up in the pack. There's a trust that makes sure every member is comfortable, regardless of income level. We've bought up a lot of land around the Pack House and created legal protections in case the state ever decides to sell off the public lands."

"That's a lot for Nora to take care of."

"She has a team of lawyers and paralegals that works for her, but most of the intricate details about how to legally protect our resources comes from her brilliant mind." Admiration tinted his tone, and Laney felt a stab of jealousy, which was stupid because Nora was brilliant.

And Laney did not want anything more from Arek than a good time in bed.

little more than an hour after they'd set off from the Pack House, the limo pulled up outside of the Villa Montalvo in Saratoga. This time, Bolt remembered to get out and open the door. Arek watched Laney gracefully slide out of the car and marveled at how she managed to navigate on the tall heels she wore. He'd meant to talk to her about their relationship during the car ride, but she'd been nervous and launching into a heavy discussion about his wolf's obsession with her seemed an extra burden she didn't need this evening. And they'd only slept together once. The beast would calm down after they'd spent some more time in bed together.

Arek wanted to punch her former department chair and dean. The possibility of one of them, or both, attending tonight plastered a grin on his face, but he'd promised Nora no public fighting. The Western Packs Coalition also wanted the matter of Inessa and her brother handled quietly. They needed to deal with Nick Novikov and his raw ambition, but no evidence led to him directly. The alphas had debated the issue for hours, and no matter how they twisted the issue and looked at it from all angles, Novikov could wrangle himself out of a formal accusation through one legal loophole or another.

The dead wolves could be rogues who acted on their own. That reflected badly on their alpha, but it happened. Inessa and her brother could be sightseeing in California. Yes, as the spouse of an alpha, Inessa should have asked permission before entering the Western territories. However, as a non-shifter, she could claim ignorance of the rules or at least claim they didn't apply to her.

On the terrace outside the villa, wealthy patrons dressed in designer labels mingled and drank champagne. Saratoga, a small community southeast of San Francisco, had the honors of qualifying as the country's most expensive suburb several times. It made sense that this place hosted an exclusive magical artifact auction. Most of the collectors could walk home at the end. The organizers marketed the event as a benefit, but Louis had done her homework and discovered that everyone counted the auction as the main attraction. The benefit provided an opportunity for the non-profit to not have to follow standard magical artifact regulations since it was all for charity.

He tucked Laney's hand under his elbow as they ascended the wide steps up to the terrace. She smiled at him, and he wanted to kiss her. The wolf's infatuation messed with his head. He needed to sort himself out if he were to hunt down the dark magic siblings. Bolt and Justice had melted into the shadows, serving as backup if needed. They counted on the dark practitioners not wanting a public spectacle. He wouldn't say he expected them to cooperate when he confronted them, but he did expect them to leave his territory and stop fucking around with his pack.

Laney took a deep breath before stepping onto the terrace.

"If Iakov is the man who abducted you," Arek said. "He will be dealt with tonight. You don't have to worry about him anymore."

She flashed him a shaky smile. "Whether he is that man or not, I'm not looking forward to meeting him."

A server approached with a tray of champagne. Arek grabbed a glass for them each. "You don't have to drink it," he said as he handed the sparkly beverage to his date. "But it helps to have something to do with your hands."

She laughed genuinely at his lame joke, a lovely sound that did weird things to his insides.

A tall slim man behind her turned around, and when he saw the source of the joy, his face lit up with recognition. "Laney," he exclaimed, and when she turned around, he pulled her into a hug. Wolf growled, maybe out loud, because his date gave him a startled look. The strange man finally stopped hugging her but rubbed her shoulders as he held her at arm's length. "You look amazing."

She did, but that wasn't any of this damn guy's business. Both Arek and Wolf agreed on that. They growled again, deep down in their throat.

Laney extracted herself from the man's grip. "Thank you, James...Oh." She stumbled a little as Arek grabbed her hand and pulled her to his side. As she found her balance, she smoothed down her skirt with her free hand, trying to free the one in Arek's grip, but he held on. She shot him a look and cleared her throat. "Have you met Arek Varg?"

The man shook his head. "No, I haven't." He smiled, but the expression didn't reach his dark eyes. Arek didn't even bother. He just returned the man's chilly gaze with his alpha stare. "You date shifters now?" The man's lip curled.

Laney ignored the man's comment and continued as if Wolf's displeased low growl didn't vibrate deep in Arek's chest. She turned to him, a fake smile on her lips. "Arek, this is James Finley. We used to work together at the university."

Finley proved to be a stupid man because instead of turning around and walking away, he said, "We were a lot more than that, Laney." His eyes never left Arek's as he chuckled without mirth. "We were about to get married."

His date shook her head. "I wouldn't go that far."

"You may not have worn my ring yet." Finley frowned. "But we talked about it."

"Did we?" Laney tugged on her hand in Arek's grip again. "That's not how I remember it." She waved her champagne glass in the air. "It's all a long time ago now." A sweet smile played on her lips.

Tug, tug.

Arek held on.

The man smelled like Laney but spicier. A mage. "Nice to meet you." Arek pulled Laney closer, draping his arm over her shoulders, without breaking eye-contact with Finley. His witch muttered something under her breath. It sounded like "testosterone," but he couldn't be sure and didn't catch the last part.

The man's eyes narrowed as he looked at Arek's arm cradling Laney. "Are you a collector, or just here to give away money?" he asked Arek, taking a sip out of his glass.

"No," he answered without specifying which question he addressed.

Laney rolled her eyes. "His role is to be eye candy tonight," she said sweetly. "I'm here to bid on my client's behalf."

Finley quirked an eyebrow. "Eye candy? Sounds like a miserable job."

Arek shrugged, sipping his champagne. Horrible stuff. The bubbles made Wolf sneeze, but Arek managed to suppress the sound. "The benefits are great." He smiled at

Laney, who rolled her eyes again. He ignored her and kissed the top of her hair.

"We should mingle," Laney said with a little laugh, but a tic spasmed in her jaw.

"Who's your client?" Finley asked.

"She can't say," Arek answered. "Confidentially agreement."

"So you don't know either."

"I know," Arek took another sip of the vile liquid in his glass and resisted the impulse to spit it out. A server passed by, and he placed the half-full glass on his tray. "I'm friends with the client." He brushed his lips against the top of Laney's hair again. "My friend introduced us." His witch muttered something under her breath. This time he couldn't hear any part of what she said, but the tone conveyed enough of the message.

"Do you have an eye on something special going up for auction tonight," Laney asked Finley.

The man smiled at her. "I wouldn't tell you if I did. I know how competitive you are." He looked back at Finley. "This lady is cutthroat. Even after we were engaged, she'd go after every promotion, every research grant that I wanted."

"Must have been hard for you to keep up," Arek said.

Laney laughed genuinely. "It was."

"That's not how I remembered it," Finley said petulantly. "I'm not the one who had to resign from my position at the university."

Laney's face clouded over, and her brow furrowed. Hurt flashed in her eyes.

Arek wanted to punch Finley but figured it would draw too much attention. Instead, he tipped Laney's face up with his knuckle under her chin and bent down to kiss her. He kept it chaste, no tongue, but left his lips on hers just a moment too long. "Their loss, my gain," he said without breaking eye contact with the sexy witch. She smiled at him. "If she hadn't left, my friend wouldn't have hired her and introduced us."

Finley cleared his throat. "I should get going."

"You should," Arek agreed. Go, Wolf growled.

Laney was startled but recovered quickly. "Good to see you, James." Her tone belied the words.

"Save me a dance?"

"No," Arek said. This guy needed to give up. Now.

Finley opened his mouth but then closed it again. He nodded to Laney and glared at Arek, who gave him the alpha stare back, knowing Wolf had turned his eyes icy-blue. The asshole caught the drift because he quickened his step as he departed.

"Was that necessary?" Laney asked, trying to shrug out of his hold around her shoulders.

"Yes," Arek said. "That guy is an ass."

"I agree, but you can't get into a pissing contest with every asshole you meet."

Could too, but he chose to keep that to himself. Instead, he swung her around so he could kiss her properly. She'd probably continue the argument later, but for now, it was an effective way to distract her.

CHAPTER 17

*L*aney shook her head once Arek stopped kissing her. "Sometimes, I'm just so happy I don't have to deal with testosterone overload. "

The pissing contest between Arek and James had been ridiculous, although she'd enjoyed certain parts. Arek seemed to instinctively push all the right buttons to set James off. Maybe all alphas knew how to do that.

"I'm happy you don't have testosterone overload as well," he shot her a sexy grin. This man confused her. How could she be delighted with him one moment, only to be infuriated by him the next? The emotional rollercoaster exhausted her, although her hormones knew exactly what they wanted.

This alpha wolf, all the time.

"What was with the growling?" she asked. The sound had reverberated deep inside her, and at first, she thought James had experienced that too, but her ex didn't react if he did, so she'd kept her own response hidden.

Arek scratched the back of his neck, his collar shifting, offering a glimpse of the platinum chain around his neck.

106

"About that...," he trailed off. His head snapped up. "Bolt's in trouble."

He grabbed her hand and dragged her behind him as he weaved between the people milling around on the terrace.

"I didn't hear anything." She had to jog to keep up with him. Grabbing the skirt of her dress, she lifted the hem so she wouldn't trip.

"The pack bonds," Arek said. "I feel his distress through the pack bonds."

They reached the corner of the terrace, and the alpha continued down the steps onto the lawn.

Laney's heels sunk into the grass. "Hold on," she sighed. "I have to take off my shoes."

Arek held her hand while she balanced on one foot and then the other, slipping off the sandals. His nostrils flared as he scented the air, eyes flashing icy blue. As soon as she'd gathered the shoes in one hand, he grabbed the other and took off again.

Soon, they'd reached the edge of the lawn where the light from the terrace didn't reach. Arek continued in a straight path into the glade of trees surrounding the lawn. Darkness clung to the trunks, and debris like leaves and branches littered the ground, making it hard for her to keep up in her bare feet. She stumbled and stubbed her toe, a small "ouch" escaping her lips.

Arek turned just as a cloud cleared the moon and pale light illuminated his face. His eyes glared icy-blue, and he tilted his head as he watched her. Something wild peaked through in his gaze. "Mate," he said with a low growl, and she knew his wolf spoke through him.

Mesmerized by the intensity in his eyes, she held her breath. Slowly she reached up to cup his face. He leaned into her touch. A sound almost like a deep purr vibrated in his chest, and she felt it echo in her own.

Suddenly, his head snapped up, and his nostrils flared. "Bolt," he said and looked down at her again.

Before she had a chance to react, he hoisted her into a fireman's carry and took off again. The ground rushed by underneath her face as she hung upside down, draped across his shoulder. His one arm looped over her thighs while the hand kept a firm grip on her butt. If the blood rushing to her had hadn't made her so dizzy, she'd admire the effectiveness of the position and how skillfully he anticipated when she'd bounce as he ran through the trees, leaping over fallen logs and low snarly undergrowth.

The terrain shifted to a hillier landscape, and she guessed they'd entered the green belt of the El Sereno Preserve adjacent to Villa Montalvo. They entered a clearing. Arek slowed down and finally stopped.

He lowered her to the ground, his gaze on her face as he did. "Are you okay?" he asked, tucking a loose tendril of her hair behind her ear. "I'm sorry. I had to get here quickly."

He'd just ran several miles, and yet his breath hadn't changed. Meanwhile, she panted heavily, and from the strands of hairs obscuring her view, she knew the elaborate hair updo that Nora had helped her with had collapsed. "It's okay," she said. "I understand." A member of the pack had called him through their bond, and his wolf had responded.

"I couldn't leave you unprotected." His azure blue gaze bore into hers. Arek had control of the wolf.

She nodded. "I know. I truly do understand." She looked around the clearing. "Where's Bolt."

A man stepped out from the trees on the opposite side. "He had to leave." He walked further out into the grassy meadow, and Laney saw his face more clearly as the moonlight illuminated his features, Iakov Aslanov.

She recognized him from the picture, and when she

reached out with magic to sample his power, she recognized it as the same as that of the man who'd abducted her. Her chest tightened, and her breath hitched.

Arek took her hand and pushed her behind him. "Where did he go?" he asked.

Iakov shrugged. "He didn't say." He kept walking toward them. The smile on his lips sent chills down Laney's spine.

Something in Arek changed. His posture remained the same, but she sensed a new intensity in him. From behind his back, she couldn't see his face, but she bet his eyes were now icy blue. The wolf had come back out.

Iakov must have noticed, too, because he hesitated for a beat before continuing his walk toward them. A few feet away, he finally stopped. He leaned to the side so he could peek around Arek and meet her gaze. "Hello again, my little witch."

Arek's wolf growled, and he sidestepped to block the mage's view of her.

Happy that she'd already removed her shoes, Laney curled her toes into the dirt connecting with mother earth. She reached out with her senses, searching for a ley line of power.

The chilly smile on Iakov's lips widened. "Ley line magic," he said. "How quaint."

Screw him. Laney tapped into the ley line she found running through the green belt. Its power flooded her senses, and she filled up the reserve she had inside her that had exactly this purpose.

This magic worked differently than when she connected with different dimensions. She'd learned this ritual when she went to mage school. She'd asked her teachers about bending of dimensions, but none of them understood what she'd tried to explain. When she'd showed them, they wrote it off as a cheap party trick, so she stopped asking questions and focused on the lessons about traditional magic-wielding instead. She'd mastered the discipline and graduated at the top of her class, but that didn't mean she stood a chance against a dark practitioner.

Arek stepped into the clearing, facing off against the mage. "What do you want?" he asked.

"I want my witch back and your pelt to round out my collection of western pack rugs," Iakov answered.

Laney gasped. Had he killed Bolt and Justice?

No, Arek would have felt it through the pack bounds and said something.

"Not going to happen," Arek growled.

"You don't really have a choice," Iakov countered. "My sister has immobilized your wolves, and there's nothing you can do about me claiming my witch."

Arek struck lightning fast. One moment he stood next to Laney. The next, he slashed the mage across the face with his hand, now shaped like a claw.

The element of surprise worked, and the mage didn't have a chance to block his strike. Deep gashes marred Iakov's face, and blood trickled down his cheek. He swiveled as Arek threw an uppercut that glanced off the mage's cheekbone instead of landing as a solid blow.

Arek crouched low and swept out with a back kick, but Iakov parried with magic.

His eyes blazed as he stretched out his arm, power shooting out from his fingertips.

Laney recognized the signature of the magic as what he'd used when he whipped her and grew tired of using the leather tool.

She screamed as Arek took the blast head on and fell to the ground.

Iakov turned to her. "Just you and me now, Little Witch."

Out of the corner of her eye, Laney saw Arek's leg twitch and his chest rise and fall.

He'd been stunned, not killed.

She exhaled in relief but kept her eyes on Iakov so he'd pay attention to her only.

The mage walked closer with gliding menacing steps.

Laney widened her stance, she probably had only one shot, and it would most likely not work, but maybe she could weaken the mage enough to where Arek stood a chance.

Behind Iakov, the air shimmered, and a grey wolf stood where Arek had lain. A pile of clothes lay in the grass beside him.

"I know you shifted," Iakov said, tilting his head to the side but not breaking eye contact with Laney. "Your beast won't protect the witch any better than your human form. She's mine to do with as I wish."

The wolf snarled. Its lips curled and pulled back from sharp teeth that glimmered in the moonlight.

Iakov turned around to face the wolf and then threw back his head, laughing loudly. "Aw, the beast has sharp little teeth. Isn't that cute?"

Laney pulled more power from the ley line. She'd already taken too much and started to feel dizzy.

The wolf stopped snarling and looked at her.

Mate?

The question whispered through her mind as Iakov raised his hands, his eyes intent on the wolf.

As he released his power, Laney screamed and channeled everything she'd stored inside. She then opened herself as a conduit with a direct connection to the ley line. Something she'd been taught over and over again never to do because it fried the practitioner. However, she couldn't think of any other way to stop a dark magic mage.

Mate.

The scream echoed loudly inside her head as a bright white light exploded inside her eyelids, and she lost consciousness.

CHAPTER 18

*A*rek came to naked and cold, lying on a rough cement floor. His head hurt like hell, and the rest of his body ached too. With a groan, he pushed off the floor and tried to stand. The world tilted, and the floor rose to smack him in the face. Before it made contact, strong arms grabbed him and lowered him until he sat solidly on his butt again.

The rim of a water bottle touched his lips, and he drank greedily.

"Easy, Boss. You're going to make yourself sick."

He opened his eyes to find Bolt bottle-feeding him as if he were a cub. Arek grabbed the bottle and hydrated himself, but he took smaller sips because his stomach cramped, proving Bolt right.

"Glad you could join the party, Mate." Justin mock saluted him from across a small square concrete cell. Both he and Bolt were as naked as himself. Not that he minded, shifters were often naked together and didn't share the same hang-ups about bodies needed to be clothed that humans seemed to have. Non-shifters seemed always to sexualize unclothed bodies. To shifters, it was just a state of not wearing fur. Although Arek did prefer not to have to fight naked and since he was in enemy territory, some covering would have been nice.

"What the hell happened?" Arek's voice sounded like gravel, and it hurt to talk. He touched his chest, looking for the familiar feel of cold platinum. Fuck, the medallion was gone.

"Don't know," Bolt answered. "I walked the perimeter of the party and then shifted so I could survey the whole parkland around the villa quickly. One moment I'm running through the park. The next, I wake up here with the worst hangover."

Arek looked at Justice and quirked a brow. Words hurt too much.

"Very similar to my story." His enforcer shrugged. "I powered off my motorbike and shifted to wolf to examine the vehicles in the parking lot for scents of dark magic. Next, I know, I wake up here with Bolt." He pointed at Arek. "You look a lot worse than how I felt when I regained consciousness. What the fuck happened to you?"

He had to think for a while before the events came to him.

Iakov in the clearing.

Laney was there too.

He tried to stand again, but the floor tilted again, and he had to sit back down. "Laney," he said. "Where's Laney?"

Bolt and Justice exchanged a look. "We don't know," Bolt said. "This cell is soundproof. So, we have no idea where we are or what's outside of here. We haven't even found a door. You just appeared in here."

No Laney, no medallion. He tried to think, but the pounding in his head kept getting worse. "Laney and I fought Iakov. She did something...," he rubbed his temples. "Fuck, I don't remember the details. I think she blasted him with magic, but I don't know. He knocked me down, so I shifted, but that's all I remember." He stood, and this time he managed to remain upright by bracing a hand against the wall. "I abandoned her with Iakov. Last time the asshole whipped her to shreds. What if she's hurt? Worse, what if she's...." He couldn't finish the sentence. Couldn't even think about Laney not being in the world.

She belonged with the living.

She belonged with him.

He swayed again.

"Hey, calm down." Bolt rushed up to hold his shoulder. "I'm sure she's fine. The little witch is resourceful, and she's survived Iakov once. She can do it again."

Arek turned and leaned his back against the wall. He couldn't stomach sitting down again. The cool cement felt better against the back of his head and shoulder than the chilly floor did on his butt. "She shouldn't have to face him alone, again. She's scared of him." In the clearing, he'd felt how frightened she was. He rubbed his chest.

"She told you that?" Justice asked, his gaze intense. "Or, you felt it?"

"She didn't tell me. I just knew." He frowned. "I mean, it would make sense that she was scared, right?"

Bolt swore under his breath. "I'm sure she's fine," he muttered. "Look, whoever has us trapped here obviously wants us alive. Otherwise, they wouldn't give us this." He held up his water bottle.

Justice turned toward Bolt. "Mate, you know that's not my point."

Bolt just shook his head.

"What is your point?" Arek asked.

"We joked around about your wolf claiming Laney, but it's

actually happened," Justice said. "If you can feel what she feels, the wolf's made her your true mate."

"No," Arek shook his head. "I mean, he's infatuated with her, but the wolf doesn't just claim a mate. It has to be a joint decision between the beast and the human." He looked between Justice and Bolt. "Doesn't it?"

"Don't look at me," Bolt clenched his fists. "I have no idea how the true mating works. Especially not with a witch."

"Fuck, Mate," Justice said. "Why are you so hung up on her being a witch?"

Bolt just shrugged. Apparently, today was the day he wanted to save all his words.

Justice turned back to face Arek. "I knew nothing about shifters—other than that I was one—until you saved us from the pits." Arek started to say that he hadn't saved them, just killed the bastard that kept them prisoner. The pitmaster needed killing because he forced people to become wolves against their will and then exploited them. Finding Bolt and Justice had been a bonus. But his enforcer waved a hand before Arek had a chance to say that. "Yeah, I know you don't think of yourself as our savior, but you are. Anyway, since I knew nothing, I've spent a lot of time reading the old stories, and there are several tales of a wolf claiming their true mate before the human side has caught up, so to speak."

Arek didn't have time to process this right now. His life was a fucking mess. He didn't have time to care for a mate. And right now, he was in a bigger mess than usual. "This sounds like something we should discuss later. We need to get out of here."

Justice sighed. "That's my whole point. You should be able to connect mentally, or at least emotionally, with Laney if she's your true mate."

Arek took a long sip of water. He finally felt well enough to stand on his own, without the help of the wall. "What if she's dead?" he finally asked. "What if I connect with her, only to find out she's been killed by Iakov. My wolf will freak out, and that's not a good thing in these close quarters." He gestured around the small cell. "I may end up killing you both." When a wolf's true mate died, the beast could go insane with grief.

But it wasn't just that.

Arek couldn't face Laney's death. He might not be able to have a relationship with her, but he needed her to be in the world. Even if she was with another man—nope, that was not something he wanted to think about. Too distracting.

The wolf growled its agreement.

"We may have to take that chance," Justice said. "I don't think your wolf will kill pack mates, no matter how rogue he goes. You may be able to ask Laney for help."

"How?" Arek said. "We have no fucking idea where we are." He turned to Bolt, "You're awfully quiet. What do you think?"

"I don't know," his second in command answered. "Can't you connect with other pack members instead? Maybe that will be safer."

Arek shook his head. "I can't communicate through the pack bond." He hesitated. How much did he want his wolves to know? They knew he could connect with them, but they may think it intrusive that he could tap into their emotions. "It's a one-way channel," he finally settled on. "I can feel your distress, but I can't send you a message."

"That's my whole point, Mate." Justice paced the small space. "An alpha that's bonded with a true mate is supposed to be able to communicate with her."

"You seem to have studied the mating bond in detail," Bolt said, his eyebrows raised.

"Most of the stories in the Pack House library are about wolves finding their mates." Justice shrugged. "I just read what was available. I guess everyone wants a happily ever after."

Arek considered Justice's suggestion. He didn't know how to handle being mated right now, but if he could, he wanted to find out if Laney was alright. He closed his eyes and reached for the bond he had with his own pack. Without the medallion, he wouldn't be able to connect with any of the other alpha's in the coalition, but he should be able to tap into the connections he had with his own wolves. He reached outward with his senses.

Justice and Bolt had a strong presence in his mind, which made sense since they were physically close to him. He could feel their distress and frustration, the feelings mirroring his own.

He extended the reach of the connection, searching for other pack members and Laney, but nothing but vast emptiness met him. Where before he'd been able to see a web of links with the rest of the pack, there was now nothing.

Frowning, he opened his eyes and stared at Justice. "I sense nothing. It's as if someone's cut off all contact between the rest of the pack and me." He gestured toward the two of them. "Except you two."

Bolt looked around the room. "Maybe this thing is shielded. Like a Faraday cage, but it blocks your alpha connection instead of E&M waves."

Arek had no idea what he talked about, but the shielding part sounded right. It felt like something blocked his pack bonds. He hadn't noticed it before, but now that he consciously thought about it, something inside him was missing.

"Well, that was a dead-end, then," Justice said. "What do we try next?"

Before Bolt or Arek had a chance to answer, one of the small cells' walls dissolved into a shimmering membrane. On the other side, a tall shape of a woman walked toward them, her features coming into focus as she got closer.

Inessa Novikov wrinkled her nose as she watched them through the transparent surface. "Of course, you'd be naked. How distasteful." She waved her hand in the air, and the three of them were clothed in jeans and white t-shirts. "Now," she said, looking straight at Arek. "My brother was supposed to be here ages ago. What the fuck have you done with Iakov?

Justice took a step closer to the shimmering wall. "Let us out, and we can discuss it."

Without breaking eye contact with Arek, Inessa twirled her index finger around.

Justice grabbed his throat, making horrible choking sounds.

"I wasn't talking to you, wolfling," the witch said. "I'm conversing with your alpha."

Arek grabbed Justice to keep him from crashing to the floor. His enforcer's face turned blue. "Release him," he shouted. "If you stop choking him, I'll tell you what happened to your brother."

Inessa quirked an eyebrow, but shrugged, and then twirled her finger in the opposite direction.

Justice gasped for air, his wolf growling loudly.

Inessa laughed. "If I wasn't pressed for time to find Iakov, I'd play with you some more, wolfling."

Bolt took a step toward her, and she snapped her head around. "You," she said, her eyebrows raised. "You taste different." She leaned closer. Her eyes focused on Bolt. "Oh, after I find my brother, I want to spend a lot of time with you." She sniffed the air, almost like a wolf. "What are you?" Her eyes widened. "You are delicious."

Bolt shuddered. Arek didn't blame him.

The woman looked deranged.

When she focused back on him, he had to steel himself from taking a step back. "Where is my brother?" the witch demanded.

Fuck. He'd had to make the lie close enough to the truth, or the dark witch would notice the deception.

CHAPTER 19

Drops of water hitting the ground made Laney open her eyes, only to be met with the gruesome sight of Iakov's head floating in the air. The drops she'd heard hitting the ground were the blood leaving his severed neck and splattering on the grass. She rolled the other way and threw up in the grass.

"Oh, shit," a woman said. "I'm sorry, I didn't mean for you to get sick. I just wanted to show you that he can't hurt you anymore."

Laney wiped her mouth with the back of her hand and turned toward the voice.

Nora squatted down and placed the dripping head on the ground. She'd been holding it by its hair. In her other hand, a curved blade glinted in the weak sun rays of dawn. It looked like a machete, and from the deep red liquid coating the steel, it was the tool she had used to behead the mage.

Laney pushed herself off the ground and to her knees. She swayed and plopped her butt on her heels for better balance. Nora reached out to grab her, but she shied away.

"I'm fine," Laney said. Nora's hand was coated in grime that she didn't want to see close up or have it touch her skin.

"Shit. Sorry, again." Nora kneeled next to Laney and wiped her hand on first the grass and then her pants.

Laney looked down at her own clothes. The beautiful dress looked like someone had dragged it across a cow pasture. A long rip down the side showed her leg from ankle to mid-thigh. "What happened?"

"That's what I was going to ask you."

Laney studied the woman, eyebrows raised. Nora had held a severed head in one hand and a bloody machete in the other, but she needed Laney to explain what had happened? She shook her head. "The last thing I remember—." Shit, Arek. What had happened to Arek? She looked past Nora, but the only thing visible in the grey light was Iakov's headless body and a pile of clothes. "Where's Arek?" she asked.

"Again," Nora said. "I was hoping you could tell me."

"Arek sensed Bolt being upset..., or something." Laney rubbed her face and then wished she hadn't when she saw how muddy her hands were. "We got to this clearing but couldn't find Bolt, only Iakov. He blasted Arek with magic, and then Arek shifted." She frowned. "I opened myself as a conduit to the ley line and hit Iakov with everything I had. That's the last thing I remember."

Nora looked over at the body lying in the grass. "Well, you got him."

"No," Laney protested. She gestured toward the head on the ground. Thankfully the eyes were closed, but the bleeding neck and the pasty skin made her want to throw up again. She swallowed down the bile. "I didn't do that."

"I know." Nora wiped the large blade on her pant leg and then slipped it behind her back between her shoulder blades and let go of the handle. "I cut off his head.

She stood and walked over to the body. Laney could see

that she wore a sheet strapped to her back. The handle of the machete peeked out from the leather. "How?" she asked.

"Hm?" Nora turned toward her. "Oh, with my blade," she said.

Laney pushed herself off the ground and felt proud when she managed to get to her feet with minimal swaying. "No," she searched for the words she wanted. "How did you know where we were, and how did you get close enough to behead Iakov?"

"The second part is easy to answer," Nora said. "I got to the clearing and saw you and Iakov both out cold on the grass. You were both breathing, which in your case was a good thing.

In his case, not so much. So, I cut his head off."

Laney blinked at her.

"Look," Nora bristled. "According to pack laws, he intruded on our territory and hurt one of our pack members. I'm totally within my rights to execute him."

"Who?" Laney asked.

"Who what?"

"Which pack member did he hurt?"

Nora's eyebrows shot to her hairline. "You. He hurt you."

"I'm not a pack member," Laney said. This conversation had gone off the rails from the very beginning, and she desperately needed it to get back on track. They needed to find Arek. They should probably get the hell away from the clearing before Inessa decided to look for her brother.

"The alpha's wolf has claimed you. Of course, you're a pack member."

"Who? What, now?" Just when she thought things couldn't get any weirder.

"You're sleeping with Arek, and it's obvious that his wolf has claimed you." Nora picked up the head by the hair, again. "We should get out of here, but I'm taking this with me so we can show Nick Novikov what happens when he sends mages to our land."

"Couldn't you just take a picture?"

"Already did," Nora said. "And I'll email that to the other coalitions' commanding alphas. To Novikov, I'll mail this head in a box. I think that will make more of a statement."

"Okay," Laney said, her mind racing as she tried to keep up with the conversation. "Can we get back to the wolf having claims on me?"

Nora walked over to the pile of clothes and picked up the beautiful tuxedo jacket that Arek had worn at the beginning of the evening. As she wrapped it around Iakov's head, Laney shuddered. That beautiful garment was now ruined forever.

"Well," the other woman said. "We should probably get out of here and try to find Arek and his lieutenants. Chances are that they hunted down Inessa." She paused and turned back to look at Laney, frowning. "Although that doesn't make any sense. Arek wouldn't have just left you here with Iakov still breathing."

"He shifted," Laney said. "Iakov's magic knocked him down, and he shifted. Maybe he ran off in wolf form." She desperately hoped that Arek had run off rather than that something horrible had happened to him.

Nora shook her head. "No, even in wolf form, he'd never leave you." She pointed toward the other end of the clearing. "Come on. I have a car parked not far from here. We'll regroup there and figure out what to do. Plus, you look like you need some water and food." She started walking.

Something glimmered in the grass next to the clothes. Laney walked over and crouched down to see better. A platinum medallion with a wolf head shaped by runes twinkled on the ground. She picked up Arek's necklace. The chain was intact. It must have slipped off his head when he shifted.

"What did you find?" Nora asked.

Laney held up the medallion. As she did, the beam of sunlight hit the platinum and reflected straight into her eyes. She looked away and gripped the piece harder so she wouldn't drop it. A current of electricity shot up her arm, and she cried out in surprise.

Her eyes teared up, and she had to close them.

All of a sudden, she saw Arek in her mind's eye.

He stood next to Justin and Bolt. They argued with a woman, but her features were out of focus, as if Laney viewed her through water.

Arek's head shot up, and he turned around. "Laney?" he whispered in her mind.

The medallion grew glowing hot, and she dropped it. A blinding headache assaulted her, and she gasped, falling to her knees.

Nora rushed to her side. "Are you okay? Do you need me to carry you to the car?" She cupped her elbow and helped Laney back up.

"I'm fine." Laney cleared her throat. "I saw Arek and the other two."

"Where?" Nora's voice grew urgent. "Did you recognize their location?"

Laney shook her head. "They were in a small room with a weird wall. They argued with a woman."

"Inessa?"

"Could be, but I can't say for sure." She reached down and picked up the medallion by its chain. "I want to try again to see if I can get a location this time."

Nora frowned. "Are you sure? It looked like the piece hurt you."

Laney nodded. "Very sure." If she could forge a connection with Arek, maybe he could tell them where he was. She steeled herself against the pain and gripped the Odin artifact again.

Holding it between her palms, she waited for the heat to sear her skin. But this time, instead of giving her a blast of hot agony, the jewelry warmed up gradually.

Laney closed her eyes, concentrating on the connection she'd felt with Arek before. No image came to her, but her hands shook, twitching. The medallion seemed attached to an invisible force that pulled her along in its wake.

She took a few steps, and the force got stronger, forcing her to jog across the clearing. She opened her eyes so she wouldn't stumble on the uneven ground.

"Hang on," Nora shouted. "That's the wrong direction from the car."

Laney tried to stop, but the invisible force pulled on her hands, and the medallion's temperature increased. When she was close to running full out, she let go of the jewelry.

The platinum medal dropped to the grass and flashed icy white.

Nora caught up with her. "I think we should get in the car and test out this little GPS. We don't know how far away they are, provided this thing guides us to Arek's location. I can run for miles in wolf form, but you don't even have shoes on." She grinned.

Laney looked down at her bare feet. They were as grimy as the rest of her. "Do you have any spare clothes in the car?"

"Of course." Nora winked. "All self-respecting shifters carry at least one change of clothes. Let's get you geared up and clothed." She picked up Iakov's head and strode through the grass. "And then we'll go and get the dark witch's head. I'm looking forward to sending Novikov a matching pair."

They reached the car, an SUV with tinted back windows and a huge cargo hold. Nora opened the back and retrieved a pack of baby wipes. She took a few out and handed the pack to Laney. "I know it's weird," the tall woman said. "But some-times I just don't want to get in the car all gory after I've hunted in wolf form or got muddy during a run." She rummaged around some more in the back of the car and held pulled out an empty cardboard box in which she deposited the tuxedo-jacket wrapped head.

Laney used the wipes to clean off as much of the mud covering her body as she could. Nora handed her a pair of black yoga pants and a pink long-sleeved t-shirt that said "Wolves Do It with a Growl" on the back. When Laney quirked an eyebrow, the lawyer just shrugged. "It was free," she said, handing over a pair of socks and trainers. "I think we have the same size."

The shoes fit perfectly. "Anything else useful in there?" Laney asked, peeking into the back of the car.

Nora grinned and opened the door wider.

Sunlight glinted off row after row of specially mounted racks filled with blades of every size imagined.

"Wow," Laney sighed. "You really like knives."

Nora sighed happily. "I do. I really do. I can't wait to test out some of these on Inessa."

CHAPTER 20

*D*izziness made Arek take a side step and stumble. He could have sworn Laney had been there with him.

He'd smelled her.

Mate, Wolf growled. *Where's Mate?*

So, it wasn't just Arek. His beast had noticed Laney's presence too. What the fuck was going on?

Bolt and Justice shot him curious looks. "Are you okay?" Bolt mouthed.

Arek nodded and mentally shook himself. He looked back at Inessa.

The dark witch had features that should make her beautiful, but her lips seemed permanently pursed in displeasure, and her eyes glittered with cruelty. The ugliness of her personality and power shone through her flawless skin. "Stop playing games, Alpha. Where is my brother?"

"He's still at Villa Montalvo," Arek said. "At least he was when I left." He cleared his throat and instantly regretted it. His throat was dry, but maybe Inessa would see it as a sign of lying. Which it wasn't, technically.

Fuck. Had he hallucinated, Laney?

Did she die, and the true mate bond—if Justice was right —had somehow messed with his head?

Bolt nudged him, and Arek turned to face him. His lieutenant gestured toward Inessa.

Oh, shit, the witch had been talking, and he'd missed whatever she'd said.

"Some persuasion seems to be needed." The witch twisted her hand.

In an instant, Justice disappeared from the cell and reappeared on the other side of the barrier, next to Inessa.

Arek clenched his jaw so hard he thought he'd crack a tooth.

"Shit," Bolt said and rammed the wall with his shoulder. It remained solid.

He launched himself against it again.

Same result.

On the other side, Justin stood frozen next to the dark witch. His eyes moved as he glared at Inessa, but the rest of his body appeared a statue.

The witch slowly walked around him, her fingernail trailing from one shoulder, across his chest, to the other shoulder, and then across his back.

She leaned in and sniffed him just above his collar bone. "Mm, tasty." She raised her head and locked eyes with Bolt. "Not as delicious as you, my friend, but all shifters have magic inside them. I'm looking forward to unlocking this one's."

Arek tried to think of something to say that would stop her from doing whatever horrible thing she was about to initiate.

Justice stared defiantly at the witch. A tic in his jaw twitching as she gripped the hem of his t-shirt and slowly lifted it to reveal his abdominal muscles and chest.

Bolt cursed and took a step back. He kicked the wall over and over again, but it didn't budge.

Inessa pulled Justice's shirt over his head. The wolf's neck muscles strained, but he still didn't move.

She placed her finger over his lips. "Shh, little wolfling. This won't hurt for very long." She giggled. "It will be pain such that you have never experienced before. But I'll keep the first burst short."

Arek joined Bolt in trying to kick down the wall, but with their bare feet, all they managed to do was hurt themselves.

The witch turned around and stared at Arek. "Watch, Alpha. See what happens to those you swore to protect when you don't do as I ask." She twisted her fingers in front of Justice's mouth, as if turning a key, and then stepped back so Bolt and Arek could see his face.

Smooth solid skin covered his lower face without a single dip or crease.

The witch had removed his mouth and nose.

Justice's eyes bulged, and his body twitched. He was suffocating.

Ice cold rage filled Arek's veins. He reached for his wolf to shift but couldn't bring the beast to the surface. His body bucked and twisted but wouldn't reshape into the wolf. Inside him, his beast howled.

Bolt watched him with horrified eyes. "I can't shift," he said. "She's stolen my wolf."

Inessa watched them both from the other side with cold eyes. "Aw, poor wolfies. Did I forget to say that you can't shift in that cell?"

Fucking dark witch. Arek would tear her from limb to limb as soon as he got out of this dammed concrete box.

In horror, he watched his enforcer's eyes roll into the back of his head.

Inessa's eyes glittered as she watched Arek seeing Justice's suffering.

Justice would die because of him because he didn't protect his people from this dark witch. Because he wasn't alpha enough to stop Inessa and Iakov from entering his territory. What kind of wolf didn't protect his pack territory?

Bolt slapped him. "What the fuck is wrong with you? We don't have time for your pity party. Justice is dying"

Had he said all those things out loud? His eyes narrowed as he looked at the witch.

She had a self-satisfied smirk on her face that convinced him she'd been messing with his head. "What kind of pathetic dark witch are you?" Anger made his voice hoarse. "I thought the bargain for giving up your soul was to become all-powerful."

Inessa frowned. "What are you babbling about, Alpha?" Behind her, Justice collapsed to the floor, but she didn't turn around, her gaze focused on Arek.

"Why can't you locate your brother yourself?" he shouted. "If you are both dark magic wielders, shouldn't you be able to find out where he is?"

"I've searched all of Villa Montalvo and the gardens," Inessa said. "I could find him anywhere, but it will take too long to search all the possible locations." She looked away. Something wasn't right about that statement, but Arek didn't have time to play games. Justice's body convulsed on the floor. He didn't have long.

"Release my lieutenant, and I'll give you a clue about where your brother is since you don't seem capable of establishing his whereabouts on your own." He smirked. "Or, does he not want to be found? Maybe he's not as fond of you as you think."

The witch waited a beat and then twitched her hand. Justice's mouth and nose returned. He drew in a long gasp of breath and then retched water on the floor.

Beside Arek, Bolt exhaled his relief.

"Hurry up, Wolf," Inessa said. "My brother is as devoted to me as I am to him. Something must have happened to him to detain him for this long. I'm sure he amused himself with your little earthbound witch, but he'd be done with her by now."

"He's in the El Sereno Preserve greenbelt," Arek said, refusing to rise to her bait. "That's where he was before you pulled me here."

The witch frowned. "Why would he go into the forest. If he wanted the earthbound witch, that's the worst place to hunt her. Her magic—." She cut herself off and studied Arek. "Where is this greenbelt in relation to the villa?"

Arek thought about misleading her but decided not to take the risk. "Straight south," he said.

A knife appeared in the witch's hand. She knelt down by Justice, who flinched but seemed not to be able to move again.

The blade flashed as Inessa swung it down, cutting the side of Justice's neck.

Bolt roared out his anger at the same time as Arek shouted, "No."

The witch rolled her eyes at them and snapped her fingers.

Justice appeared back in the cell. Arek pulled off his shirt and applied it to Justice's neck to stanch the flow of blood.

His enforcer whispered, "Mate, that witch is so far beyond wicked. She's straight-up evil."

"Don't talk," Arek said, pressing against the wound. He took a deep breath as the blood flow slowed down and eventually stopped. The cut hadn't been deep.

Meanwhile, the dark witch knelt with the bloody blade held out in front of her in both hands. She raised her arms so that the knife tip was above her head and tilted her head back. Blood slowly dripped from the metal down into her mouth.

Bolt gagged.

Arek didn't blame him. He didn't mind the taste of raw blood during the full moon hunt or even when he tore into an enemy while in wolf form. But the witch seemed to revel in its taste. She hummed and swayed as the red drops flowed into her mouth.

Gross.

Her head snapped forward, and her eyes rolled into the back of her head so that only the whites showed.

"Fucking evil, I say," Justice whispered.

"This is why I don't like witches," Bolt muttered.

Laney was nothing like this deranged woman, and Arek was about to tell him that when an inhuman wail assaulted his eardrums.

The witch's eyes snapped back, fury blazing out of them as she locked gazes with Arek. "You killed him," she shrieked. "You and your fucking witch beheaded him and left his body to rot in the forest."

Fuck.

Whatever deranged vision she had seen, it meant very bad news for him and his wolves.

"Incoming," Justice shouted as Inessa rose and launched herself at them, the bloody knife held high, dripping onto her dress.

The transparent wall that had been indestructible when Arek and Bolt had tried to get to Justice shimmered one last time and disappeared.

The three wolves immediately took a step outside the cement prison cell, ripped off their clothes, and shifted.

If the barrier between them and the deranged dark witch was down, facing her as wolves was the better option.

Perhaps the only option if they were to survive.

CHAPTER 21

*N*ora drove the way she beheaded people, sharply and decisively, but with a lot of mess left in the wake.

"You just ran that stop sign," Laney said, looking behind them. The horns of the other cars grew distant as Nora sped them away from the intersection.

"Don't worry about how I drive," the lawyer said. "Concentrate on where I'm supposed to go."

Laney thought about pointing out the contradiction in that statement but instead closed her eyes and focused on the tugs and pulls that indicated which way the medallion wanted them to go.

She held the artifact cupped in her palms. That way, the heat of the metal didn't bother her as much as when she squeezed it between her hands. The jewelry glowed and gave off a blaze of heat that increased the further they drove.

"Turn left," she told Nora without opening her eyes but winced when she heard the squealing of rubber against asphalt.

Nora probably took the corner on two wheels and,

judging from the angry honking, cut off a few other cars in the process. They'd been heading south on highway nine and were now going west on highway seventeen, heading into the Santa Cruz Mountain foothills, toward the Lexington Reservoir.

The medallion's temperature increased, and Laney had to take deep breaths as it burnt her skin again.

"You okay," Nora asked, squeezing her knee. As the other woman's touched her, the metal of the jewelry cooled while the pull on Laney's hand became stronger.

"Keep doing that," she said.

"Keep doing what?"

"Touching me. I don't know why, but it focuses the medallion."

Nora did as asked, and now Laney could see images in her mind. "They're in a garage or something that's used to store vehicles." She frowned. "I can't get a clear picture of the outside, but the inside is mostly concrete." She paused, focusing on the images broadcasting in her mind. "And it's close to water. On the shore of a large body of water."

"Could it be a fire station?" Nora asked. "There forestry service has a station right on the edge of the reservoir."

"Yes," Laney said when Nora's words clarified the images in her head. "There are several buildings and a helicopter pad."

"That's it. I know exactly where that is." The lawyer pushed down the gas pedal, and the SUV shot forward.

Laney dropped the medallion and grabbed the door handle to stay in the seat. She gasped as Nora crashed through a pair of metal-framed chicken wire gates without slowing down and continued down a driveway. They sped through a deserted parking lot.

"This station is in use," the lawyer said. "There should be people and cars here at all hours."

"Inessa could have used dark magic to convince them all to go home," Laney said. The car had finally slowed down enough to where she could reach for the medallion on the floor. As soon as she grabbed it, she got a flash of Arek. He'd shifted to wolf. "There," she pointed to a building with big bay doors. "That's where they are."

Nora punched the gas pedal again and drove straight through the bay doors. They crumpled with horrible noises of grinding metal and shattering glass.

The SUV skidded sideways before the lawyer got it under control and stood on the break.

The squeal of tires against concrete reached Laney's ears at the same time as the stench of burning rubber invaded her nose.

She paid it no attention, though, because her eyes were on the drama unfolding in front of her, inside the station.

Three wolves faced off against Inessa. They hunched low, their lips pulled back in snarls, as they advanced on the dark witch.

Laney recognized Arek's grey wolf and Bolt's silver. The gray and brown brindle had to be Justice.

Nora jumped out of the car, slamming the door behind her. "Hello, boys, did you miss me?" She pulled the machete from the sheet strapped to her back. "I want the witch's head. It goes with the one I have in the back of the car."

Inessa shrieked and turned away from the wolves, advancing toward Nora instead. "You killed my brother."

"I did," Nora said, holding her blade with both hands in front of her. She widened her stance and rotated her shoulders. "What are you going to do about it?"

Laney wanted to tell her to stop taunting the dark witch. Inessa didn't need proximity to strike, but then she saw that the wolves had advanced behind the dark witch while she'd been distracted by Nora. The lawyer had drawn the witch's attention on purpose.

Laney jumped out of the car and slipped the medallion around her neck. She didn't know why, but it had been her guiding talisman, and so she'd rather have it with her than leave it in the car.

The silver wolf rushed the witch and jumped. His fangs sunk deep into her neck, and he snarled as he tore at her skin.

Inessa clapped her hands together, and an invisible wind blew the wolf away from her, slamming him into the wall.

He whimpered as he slid down on the floor, one of the hind legs at an awkward angle.

Laney closed her eyes and reached out with her senses, looking for a ley line. She wasn't sure she could pull on the magic after opening herself wide as a conduit when she blasted Iakov. Her system might be fried. But she felt the familiar pull and found a strong current of magic running down the middle of the reservoir. The combination of running water above a ley line made it easier to tap into the power, and she drew from the clean earthbound energy, feeling rejuvenated in a way she'd never experienced.

Suddenly, the dark witch turned her way and focused her cruel cold eyes on Laney. "Oh no, you don't get to pull on your feeble earthbound power," she hissed. "It's your fault my brother is dead. If he hadn't chased after you, we'd have slaughtered and skinned the alpha and his two lieutenants by now." She took a step toward Laney. "And I'd be sketching designs of a fur coat for my tailor."

Arek's wolf snarled and placed himself in front of Laney, a growling, pawing barrier of muscle and fur between her and the dark witch. In wolf form, Arek was the size of a small pony.

"Hello," Nora called. "I'm the one who cut your brother's

ugly head." She held out the machete. "Want to touch the blade that severed his neck?"

Inessa kept her gaze locked with Laney's but flicked her hand toward the lawyer. A blast of power punched Nora backward and into the grill of the SUV. She cried out and crumpled to the floor.

The brindle wolf ran over to her and nudged her with his nose. He whimpered when Nora didn't move.

The dark witch kept advancing on Laney, who gathered her power around her. She knew she couldn't open herself up as a conduit again, not if she wanted to survive. Filling her inside well with magic was already more effort than usual. She swayed on her feet and grabbed on to Arek for support.

As her hand made contact with his pelt, the medallion around her neck blazed blinding white. The overhead lights all popped one-by-one. Glass rained down as sparks of electricity sizzled in the air.

Power of a strength Laney had never felt before flowed through her body, filling her reserves to the brim, and still, she could pull in more without overloading her senses.

The grey wolf turned to look at her with icy-blue eyes. *Do you feel this?* Arek's voice asked in her head.

Yes, she answered through the connection which he had spoken and pulled in even more power.

Inessa raised her hands, sparks of magic arching between her palms to form a glowing neon green ball. Her lips moved, but Laney couldn't make out what spell the dark witch chanted. She probably wouldn't recognize it if she could.

The green ball grew in size, and Laney pushed everything she had into a magical shield she erected to hopefully protect herself and Arek from Inessa's incoming assault. The wolf crouched down as if preparing to leap.

Don't, Laney sent down their connection. *I can't hold the shield if you jump through it.*

The wolf growled and pawed at the ground, but some of the tension left its body.

Inessa palmed the ball in one hand and raised it higher.

She threw the glowing globe of power toward Laney, who pushed everything she had into the shield she'd constructed.

A loud bang reverberated through the building as a blaze of green light blinded Laney. She closed her eyes against the intensity of the flare.

When she opened them again, Inessa had vanished, and a stench of burning hair lingered in the air.

The grey wolf wrinkled its nose and sneezed. *Are you okay?* Arek's voice asked in her head.

She nodded.

On the other side of the garage, a naked Bolt sat up. He groaned as he held his head. "Fucking witch ran away scared."

Justice had also shifted and kneeled next to Nora. "Her breathing is steady," he called out. "She's going to have one hell of a concussion, but I think she's going to be okay.

Laney looked around the room. The bay doors were completely demolished. Shattered glass covered every surface, and several of the lights hung onto the ceiling by only a wire or two.

The firefighters and forestry personnel were in for a surprise when they came into work in the morning.

EPILOGUE

The afternoon sun warmed his skin as Arek walked across the lawn to the back terrace where Laney sat with one of his old ledgers.

The last few days had been busy. They'd cleared out of the fire station without getting noticed. The local paper had reported that a freak tornado must have touched down on the edge of Lexington Reservoir but destroyed only one building, leaving the others intact.

Arek had arranged for a large anonymous donation that should take care of all the damage and still leave enough for a new fire engine or two.

Bolt's leg had healed perfectly the next time he shifted into wolf. Nora's concussion hadn't been as easy to fix, but with rest, she should also recover completely. She looked forward to mailing Iakov's head to the Novikovs. Unfortunately, that would probably never happen.

He frowned, thinking of the conference video call he'd just completed with the alphas of the Western Pack Coalition. Arek had been all for shipping the gruesome package to

Nick and Inessa, but the council requested a less overt gesture of aggression.

However, by the end of the meeting, there'd been no clear decision of what action to take. The alphas wanted more discussion. Arek didn't see why. The Novikovs had trespassed in his territory. They needed to be dealt with swiftly, or they'd keep violating the Pack Directives.

But that was a worry for another day. He'd rarely seen Laney during these few days, and the two hadn't had a chance to really talk. Something he wanted to rectify right away.

He climbed the two steps up to the patio and approached the table where she sat. "Mind if I join you?"

She looked up, shielding her eyes against the sun with one hand. "No," she said, smiling, but it was tentative.

He knew how she felt. The speaking mind-to-mind had been freaky. He'd tried to repeat it but hadn't been successful. It probably only worked when they had physical contact.

Arek pulled out a chair and sat. He cleared his throat. "How's the cataloging going?"

"I'm making progress." She pushed her hair away from her face. "But it's going to take a long time to get it all organized."

"Does that mean you'll stay for a while?" He liked the idea of her staying in the house for a long time.

She hesitated. "You mean, live here? Or, do you mean just work here?"

He tried to read her face to see which option she preferred, but he couldn't tell. Her amber eyes calmly met his, although, from the pulse in her neck beating rapidly, he knew she wasn't as serene as she pretended to be. Still, it didn't give him a clue as to which choice she'd rather make. "Whatever you are comfortable with," he finally said, grabbing her hand and pulling it toward him.

No, Wolf growled. *Mate lives here.*

Laney jumped. "Was that what...who I think it was?"

Arek nodded, watching her carefully for any signs of fear. "Yeah, he likes to butt in at the most inconvenient times."

She tilted her head. "I could hear him in my mind, just like we talked to each other at the fire station."

"Did that scare you?"

"Which one?"

"Either." He held his breath, waiting for her answer. There was no doubt that they were true mates, but he didn't want to force something on her that she wasn't prepared for.

She paused for a beat. "No," she finally said. "It's interesting. A little weird. But not scary."

"So this thing with the wolf." He paused.

"Nora says you and I are true mates." Laney pulled her hand back, and he immediately missed the contact.

"She's right." He cleared his throat. "How do you feel about that?"

She searched his face. "How do you feel about that?"

He smiled. Answering a question with a question was his favorite evasive move. "I honestly don't know." He grabbed her hand again. "It's sudden and strange. But yet, it somehow feels right."

"Yeah," she whispered and then cleared her throat. "Nora also said that wolves mate for life and go insane if their true mate dies or abandons them."

"Nora has a lot to say on the subject."

"I kind of asked her about it." Laney smiled. "According to her, I interrogated her."

He reached for her other hand, holding both in his. "I don't want you to feel pressured into anything." He wanted her to stay, but not if it wasn't her choice.

"What do you want?" she asked. "Tell me how you see this working?"

He laughed. "I have no freaking idea. But I know I want you here, with me, while we figure out how this can work for both of us."

Her smile lit up his heart. "I like that," she said. "I like that very much."

Mate stays, Wolf purred.

Laney giggled.

Stupid beast. Always had to have the last word.

Arek leaned over the table and claimed his mate's lips.

For once, the wolf remained quiet.

THANK you for reading this book! Do you want to know what's next for The Norse Billionaire Shifters? *A Wolf's Obsession* (Bolt's book) will be out this summer, and *A Wolf's Craving* (Justice's book) arrives early fall. Both are available for pre-order now.

Join my VIP Readers List to gain access to exclusive content and giveaways:
www.asamariabradley.com/newsletter/

A WOLF'S DESIRE SHORT STORY

In 2020, I entered The Who's Your Prince? 1,001 Dark Nights Short Story Challenge. To my delight, I was selected as one of the winners. All the winning stories became the 1,001 Dark Nights Short Story Anthology 2020 that was available free across all retailers for three months. I can't tell you how honored and proud I was to be a part of this collection and how grateful I am to Liz Berry, Jillian Stein, and MJ Rose for running the contest. Without them, there would be no Norse Billionaire Shifters series.

As a special bonus for purchasing the print version of the book, turn the page for the very beginning of The Norse Billionaire Shifters series.

Enjoy!
-Asa

A WOLF'S DESIRE

Thirty years ago, wolf shifter and self-made billionaire Magnus Flink challenged and killed his sadistic alpha to stop him from torturing and murdering pack members. He's been a rogue ever since and wants nothing to do with pack politics. But now, a war is brewing between the four major shifter coalitions. And when a power-hungry alpha wields dark magic to kidnap the woman Magnus's wolf has claimed as mate, he'll have to stretch the limits of his abilities—animal and human—to save her.

CHAPTER 1

*M*agnus Flink adjusted the collar of his tuxedo shirt and wished he could undo the top button, but that would make his bowtie lopsided. As much as he hated formal dress, the tux was more than just clothing in this environment. It was protection.

The members of Denver's high society, currently mingling in the lobby of the Museum of Art, pretended to be the closest of friends, but any fashion faux pas counted as a chink in one's armor. Magnus never showed weakness.

As a shifter, the wolf inside him wouldn't allow it.

A server passed by with a tray of champagne glasses, and Magnus grabbed one. His metabolism burned alcohol too fast for it to have any effect, but holding a skimpy glass of the piss-colored liquid was better than skulking around with clenched fists as he navigated the tall tables dotted around the marble-floored lobby for yet another charity auction.

Passing three beautiful women, he smiled politely. The blonde in the middle gave him a once over, which he ignored. Instead, he stayed on course toward the back of the room. He was here for one reason only: to chase down the woman his wolf had decided would be their mate.

He found an empty table by a wall, which he leaned against as he surveyed the crowd. Another couple of women, and one of the men, glanced his way appreciatively. He knew people found him attractive, but it wasn't just because of his looks. You could dress up any thug in an expensive tux, and people would faun all over him.

And thinking of ugly thugs, here was one now. The commanding alpha of the Western Packs, Arek Varg, entered the venue, scanned the room, and then set a course straight for Magnus. He sighed inwardly and resisted the urge to escape. Wolf called to wolf. There was no way to hide from a fellow shifter.

Arek plowed through the crowd, his piercing sky-blue eyes even more intense than usual. Dressed in a black button-down shirt tucked into slacks, also black, he looked underdressed.

"Nice outfit," Magnus said when Arek walked up. "Shouldn't an alpha dress better to the occasion?"

The other shifter stepped to the opposite side of the table and put his back against the wall. "I didn't pack a monkey suit because I didn't know I'd have to track you down at a circus." His disdain showed clearly on his face as he looked around the room. "Why aren't you answering calls or texts?"

Magnus shrugged. "I'm busy." He stared at the ancient platinum medallion Arek wore instead of a tie. It was a wolf head inscribed with runes, with three interlocking triangles on its forehead. The triangles symbolized Odin. Like Magnus, the alpha had been born in Scandinavia, but several decades before himself. Rumors said the medallion had magical powers.

Magnus met the alpha's hard gaze—because he could. His wolf was dominant enough to do so. One day they'd probably brawl to see who was more powerful. Not this evening, when regular humans could get hurt, however. "I didn't know you were in town."

A muscle in Arek's jaw visibly tightened. "If you'd picked up your phone, you'd know," he growled.

Magnus's wolf rose in response to the anger permeating the air. He faked calm, even though he knew Arek would notice his beast. "Right."

Arek glared at him for a few beats. His eyes lightened to the icy-blue color of his wolf's gaze. "Don't fuck with me. I'm in no mood for games."

Fury drove Magnus's beast even closer to the surface. His eyes would now be yellow, and he aimed that sulfur-colored gaze at Arek. "Games?" he breathed out in a low growl. "*I'm playing games?*" He laughed bitterly. "You are the one who likes political bullshit. I refused all that when I declined the alpha role in my old pack." He tilted his head, still locking gazes with Arek.

The shifter returned the stare. "True, but remaining rogue is now impossible."

Magnus sighed. "I've heard that before, remember?" The packs of the United States had during the last two decades formed larger coalitions. There were four Commanding Alphas. Arek actually cared about his packs, but Magnus had a healthy distrust of authority. He'd once sworn fealty to an alpha, which turned out to be a disastrous decision.

Suddenly, his wolf clamored for attention, and he looked around the room for the source of the beast's agitation.

Jasmina Parker stood at the bar, dressed in a short red dress that hugged her delectable curves in all the right places. Her sculpted legs went on for miles before ending in a pair of strappy heels that made his mouth water. The overhead spotlights revealed red highlights in her shoulder-length light brown hair.

"I know you want to remain unpledged due to your...bad experience." Arek relaxed and his eyes returned to their usual deep blue.

"That's one way of describing it." Magnus would characterize it as being tortured by a deranged sadistic alpha, but he'd lost the thread of the conversation because his wolf wanted—needed—to go see Jasmina.

Arek cleared his throat. "You've been rogue for decades now. It's not good for your wolf. You need pack ties to help calm him. I can see that he is almost controlling you."

He was right. The wolf was on high alert, but that was all Jasmina's fault. A hundred pack mates singing lullabies would not calm the beast with her in the room. He'd been obsessed with her from day one, but she'd turned away from him each time. However, he could sense her interest, and it was time to let his wolf have free rein. Magnus pushed the glass of now warm champagne to the center of the table. "Talk to you later," he said.

Arek grabbed his jacket sleeve before he could leave. "We are on the precipice of major changes. Dangerous changes. You cannot ignore this."

Magnus snarled but took a breath when he saw Arek's earnest expression. "We'll have breakfast tomorrow." He had to eat anyway. Discussing pack politics would suck, but agreeing to talk would get him quicker to where he needed to be.

Next to the woman in the red dress.

CHAPTER 2

*M*ina waited for the bartender to mix her gin and tonic. She needed fortification for the tedious evening ahead. Her new position at the magazine's Lifestyle section meant she now wrote fluff pieces about Denver's rich and beautiful instead of the hard-core investigative pieces she'd been hired to do. All because she'd been put in an impossible situation and refused to compromise her ethics.

Technically, she didn't even have to attend this event to write about it. She had a copy of the guest list and the organizer had promised to email her the auction results. The magazine's photographer would take care of the visuals for the piece. But her editor believed in giving the readers an "in the moment" experience. So here Mina was, eavesdropping on the rich and entitled so she could pepper the article with gossip.

The bartender finally finished making her drink. She was about to start mingling when a sizzle of awareness trailed down her spine.

Only one man ever caused that reaction. As if she'd

conjured him out of her hot dreams, there he was. Self-made billionaire Magnus Flink. CEO of Dold, the most high-earning software security company in the United States, and voted Denver's most eligible bachelor.

But it wasn't his square chin, sexy dimples, taut body, or vast fortune that made him haunt her dreams. It was the aura of danger that clung to him. She'd always been a sucker for bad boys, and *this* bad boy in *that* tux had her hormones salivating.

Too bad he was the reason she now wrote articles that made her search the thesaurus for adjectives to describe rich people's outfits.

"Jasmina Parker." His deep tone did funny things to her insides, but she ignored that. At least she tried to. Flink ordered a beer and then aimed his emerald green gaze on her. "On assignment for another riveting piece about our city's elite?"

She pasted a fake sunny smile on her lips. "I've told you before that I prefer Mina, but yes, I am. What kind of art does Denver's most eligible bachelor prefer?"

His face clouded over as he grabbed the beer from the bartender and tipped generously. Flink had been grouchy the whole time she'd interviewed him for the bachelor article. If the contest hadn't been to raise money for a homeless shelter, she doubted he'd have participated.

After that interview, she'd run into him at a few events. She always reacted with this hot, sizzling, instant sexual attraction that made her body hum in pleasure. The worst part was with a shifter's power of scent, he knew his effect on her.

And that was the crux of the problem. Mina *knew* he hid a wolf inside him, and she'd nearly been killed by one of his kind. No matter how sexy Flink was, she'd never put herself in that position again.

The eligible bachelor interview had been for a good cause, but it had also been a cover to get close to Flink. Her editor wanted an in-depth article about how the billionaire had built his company and massive fortune. And she did find out, but had she written that he had been alive in the early days of computers—and yes, even when the term referred to humans doing calculations—her editor would have demanded she take a few weeks off, maybe years.

She'd dated a guy in college who hid a wolf inside him. When Flink's eyes had turned yellow because the photographer wanted yet another pose, she'd recognized him as a shifter, and the danger he posed to her.

Flink turned toward her now, a polite smile on his lips. "My tastes? I like all beautiful creations." Although his gaze never left hers, her nerve endings told her he slowly perused her body all the way down and then up again.

Her nipples tightened in response, or maybe that was just because he stood so close his body heat enfolded her. A blush heated her cheeks, and she looked down, fiddling with the straw in her glass. "I'm sure you'll find many examples of beauty here tonight. Although many of the people have expressions as stiff as the portraits on the wall, because of Botox."

His smile deepened into something more genuine. He cupped Mina's elbow, steering her toward a table in the corner. Two other men were also heading that way, but a look from Flink had them quickly changing direction. "Seriously, why are you writing about high society?"

Mina put her drink on the table and next to it, placed her small evening purse. "I write about whatever my editor assigns me."

He positioned himself with his back toward the wall, and yet his body sheltered her from the crowd. "Your editor is an idiot. I've read some of your articles."

She ignored the warmth spreading through her body at his unintentional compliment. "You googled me?"

He leaned forward, elbows on the table. "I research everyone writing about me." Foolish her for thinking she was special. "What happened that made your assignments change?"

Mina thought about giving the official spiel about new career opportunities and challenges, but her feet already hurt in the ridiculous high strappy sandals she'd chosen to wear.

For him. In case he'd be here.

Her hormones made her do it, and she couldn't hide her reaction any longer. It was obvious he knew she was attracted to him, so she might as well give him the truth and tell him to get lost. She lifted one leg and rotated her foot to relieve her squashed toes. "You happened."

"I caused your demotion?" His eyebrows rose.

"My editor wanted to find out why you are leagues ahead of your competitors, both in technology and earnings. He suspects something illegal."

Flink shook his head. "He demoted you when you told him my success is due to only hard work and determination?"

"Oh no, I found the real reason for your prosperity." She sucked down the rest of her drink. "You have personal knowledge of all historical computer research. Of course, nobody would believe me if I wrote that. I refuse to report lies, so I had to refuse the assignment."

Flink laughed. "Personal knowledge? You think I'm immortal?"

"No, but wolf shifters live a very long time."

"I'm a werewolf?" His voice lowered, and his eyes shifted from green to honey-color. His wolf observed her now. "Aren't you a little too old for fairy tales?"

Even people who didn't know shifters walked among

them would instinctively flee from that yellow gaze. But she'd battled one big bad wolf already, so she leaned closer. "You can growl your denial all you want, but when your eyes turn yellow, I see the beast inside you."

His eyebrows rose, and then he smiled. "Come home with me."

Her body screamed yes. She ignored it. "I prefer to know my lovers on an emotional level before we have sex."

He tilted his head. A very wolf-like gesture. "Does emotional closeness always have to proceed physical intimacy? Could a relationship not start the other way around?"

"Does that line ever work?"

"You tell me. I've never tried it on anyone else." His eyes were back to emerald green.

Mina believed him, and she actually had no problem with causal sex. However, in this case, fantasizing about how hot the two of them would be together would have to be enough.

Her ex-boyfriend had turned obsessively jealous and had for days physically restrained her to stop her from leaving his house. He couldn't help it, because his wolf had decided she was its mate. Dating a shifter was not an experience she would repeat.

"I've had a long day and am too tired for this game. Have a pleasant evening." She picked up her bag and walked toward the exit.

CHAPTER 3

*A*fter the cold air conditioning inside the museum's lobby, Mina relished the warm summer night air that caressed her bare shoulders. The weather report had promised a balmy evening, so she hadn't bothered with a coat. The way the close proximity to one hot wolf in a killer tuxedo had overheated her body, she wouldn't have needed one even if the season had been an extra frigid Colorado winter. She took out her phone and opened the ride-share app.

Fast steps behind her had her turning around quickly with her breath held.

Flink slowed his steps as he got closer and grabbed her hand. "I don't want to part on bad terms." His callused palm felt warm against hers.

"We didn't." She resumed breathing and tried to free herself.

He held on. "Give me a few moments." He stepped off the curb and tugged her with him. "I need to—"

The loud laugher of a group leaving the event interrupted him.

He pulled her with him as he stepped into a narrow alley between two buildings. The light from the glass walls of the lobby barely reached into the shadows but illuminated his face enough to where she could see his serious expression. "We need to talk."

Mina shook her head. "I don't think that is a good idea." She tugged on her hand again. This time he let go, but she didn't leave. She stood there, waiting for something, but she didn't know what.

"If you won't listen to words, maybe this will get your attention." He bracketed her face with his palms. "I've been wanting to do this for months," he whispered as he leaned in and captured her lips with his.

Mina closed her eyes and savored the kiss she'd pictured in her mind so many times. His firm lips slowly explored hers. She leaned into him. This was madness, but she'd been wondering for months what this would be like.

He tilted his head and increased the pressure of the kiss, demanding more access.

When she yielded, he groaned, and his tongue thrust into her mouth.

Her body ignited, and she pressed closer.

A moan escaped her as his hands slid down her back, pushing so that her heat met his hardness. Mina tugged on the collar of his shirt. She needed more.

She needed *him*.

Her nipples brushed against the structured fabric of his jacket, sending sizzles of pleasure straight to her core. Her eyes flew open, and she struggled to catch her breath. "This is crazy. We're outside. Anyone could see us."

She lost interest in their location when he buried his hands in her hair, tilting her head to deepen the kiss, and then those clever lips traced kisses along her jaw and down her neck. She sighed with pleasure and closed her eyes again as he went lower and sucked on her collarbone.

"More," she murmured, pulling on his collar again, but Flink resisted—a little too much. She opened her eyes and leaned back. His jaw clenched, but his body remained as still as a marble statue. "What's going on?"

His eyes turned honey-colored and focused on something behind her. A low growl rumbled in his throat.

Arms of steel grabbed her from behind, banded around her middle and neck, and pressed her against a hard chest. "This is a sweet treat," an accented voice said. She couldn't tell if it was Russian or Eastern European. "I may have a little taste myself before I hand her over to the boss."

Anger distorted Magnus' face, and a muscle pulsed in his jaw, but his body remained frozen.

Mina fought against the man. His grip wouldn't budge. Instead, he increased the pressure around her neck, forcing her chin up as she struggled for breath.

Helpless, she stared at Magnus, whose eyes glared at her captor.

The man dragged her deeper into the alley. Mina relaxed all her muscles, but becoming deadweight just increased the pressure against her throat, cutting off her oxygen.

He dragged her around the building to a car parked beneath an overhang. When he had to use the arm holding her around her waist to open the door, she fought with all her might, scratching his arm and kicking his shin.

She stomped her heel on his instep.

The attacker shouted in a foreign language but renewed his grip around her waist so roughly that she lost her footing. She went down in a heap on the ground, dragging the man with her. The asphalt scraped the skin on her bare legs, but Mina ignored the pain and scrambled, trying to get away.

She felt the man's fingers in her hair, pulling hard, and then slamming her head into the pavement.

Everything went black.

CHAPTER 4

*F*our hundred and eighty seconds.

Eight fucking minutes.

That's how long it took for whatever had frozen Magnus to lose its hold. He'd been counting every tick of the Breguet watch on his wrist. By the time he'd run down the alley to where the shifter had dragged Jasmina, they were long gone. There wasn't even a scent trail to follow.

He raked his hand through his hair. There had been a thud and Jasmina's screams had cut off. If that fucker had hurt her... he had to swallow the bile that rose in his throat.

How had the bastard cloaked himself from Magnus's senses? And what in the hell had he used to freeze him? He'd lost complete control of his muscles and could only watch as the fucker dragged Jasmina, *his* Mina, down the alley.

If the shifter used some kind of paralyzing agent, Magnus couldn't risk Mina's safety by going after him alone. Backup was needed. Grabbing his phone, he dialed the number that was listed several times in his recent calls log.

Arek answered on the third ring. "A little early for breakfast. I haven't even gone to bed yet." Loud music played in the background.

"I need your help," Magnus bit out. "I'm outside the Museum of Art." He hung up before Arek wasted time by asking questions.

Pacing the alley, he again counted seconds. His wolf wanted them to shift so they could go hunting, but without a trail, there was no use. Why had the Russian wolf targeted Mina? She knew something about the shifter world, but he doubted a regular human would be involved in pack politics.

After five hundred and ninety-two seconds, Arek finally arrived. "I was at a bar on the other side of downtown. They had a really good band—"

"No time for chit chat," Magnus growled.

Arek's eyes lightened, but he asked in a calm voice, "What happened?"

Magnus described Mina's abduction.

"Russian accent," Arek said. "That could be one of Novikov's wolfs."

"The second of the New York pack?" Magnus shook his head. "Why would he kidnap Mina?"

The other shifter sighed. "This is why I am here. Novikov challenged his alpha last year and won. He's now the commanding alpha of the Eastern Packs, and he has ambitions to expand into the Midwest."

"The alpha in charge of the central regions is one of the strongest wolves alive. Novikov can't defeat him."

"With the help of his new wife he can," Arek answered. "He's married a dark witch."

"Fuck." Magic fueled by blood sacrifices had rendered him immobile. His former alpha had dabbled in that shit. "Why would he take Mina?" He paced again.

"Because you were with her." Arek sat down on one of the couches. "This is what I've been trying to talk to you about.

Novikov is about to start, if not a war, a major conflict. He's going to use your woman to pressure you into joining his pack."

"And thereby force me to pay him tithing." Each pack member paid a percentage of their income to the pack. The money was supposedly for expenses like those of the full moon hunt, but some packs purchased weapons and fortifications.

"Exactly," Arek answered. "With your wealth and his wife's skills, he'll be able to take over a good chunk of the US, if not all of it."

Magnus would pay anything to get Mina back, but handing over money to someone that resorted to kidnapping did not give him confidence that they would return her unhurt, or at all. "We have to find them before they leave Denver." He looked at Arek's medallion. "Can you use your magic jewelry?"

The other shifter's lips stretched into a wry smile. "Don't tell me you believe those stupid rumors." He grasped the medallion. "This was my grandfather's. It works as a focus to tap into the mental connections I have with my pack, but only because it has value to me. It is worth nothing in monetary terms." He put his hand on Magnus's arm. "I doubt Novikov's wolf will drive all the way back to New York. He probably has a private plane waiting somewhere."

Magnus walked toward the museum parking lot. "The metropolitan area of Denver has four municipal airports. Five if we count Boulder." He patted his pockets for the keys to his Tesla Model S. "Centennial is south of here, but all the others are north, so let's head that way."

Suddenly, his wolf gave alert for—not danger exactly—but it insisted on taking over his senses the way it did when they were hunting. Magnus had learned the hard way to pay attention to his wolf, and this was something new. He stopped.

Arek, who'd been following closely, almost smacked in to him. "What's going on?"

"I don't know. The wolf is trying to tell me something." He closed his eyes. "It's like when it has picked up a scent trail, but it is not quite that."

"Are you bonded to your woman?" the older wolf asked.

"She's not exactly my woman," Magnus said. "The wolf has decided he wants her, that's all." Although he had kissed her. Touched her.

"Maybe he can find her."

Magnus tossed him the key fob. "You drive, and I'll concentrate on whatever the wolf is trying to tell me."

Arek grinned when he saw what car unlocked when he pressed the button. "I've always wanted to drive one of these."

Magnus' beast sent images and impressions so quickly he couldn't keep up. He slid into the passenger seat. The double vision of the road that the Tesla traveled on, and the journey the wolf seemed to be on, made him close his eyes. The beast became more agitated.

"I'm just heading north on I-25 and hope you'll tell me if, or when, I have to exit," Arek said.

Magnus' wolf provided scents, sounds, and images through their connection. But it wasn't anything Magnus could translate into driving directions.

The wolf told him they'd once chased a bunny across soft grass nearby Mina's current location, but Magnus had run in wolf form in most of Denver's urban green areas and the surrounding beautiful wilderness.

Finally, the beast sent something that made sense. A store that made wooden furniture that smelled like actual trees.

"They're heading for Erie Airport." Magnus gave Arek

directions. Thank goodness he'd shopped for a custom-made barn door a few weeks ago.

The alpha pressed down on the gas pedal, and twenty minutes later, they reached the small municipal airport north of Denver. Dawn lightened the sky in the west as they parked half a mile from the official lot.

Both of them shifted to wolf. Being fully one with his animal freed something inside Magnus. Feelings not his own flooded his senses.

Mina's feelings.

She was angry—no, furious.

He took lead as they ran toward a small jet on the runway that looked ready to take off. Sounds of struggle came from inside the plane.

They were still fifty yards away from the aircraft when a muffled banging erupted, and the door flew open, revealing Mina tumbling to the ground and landing in a controlled tuck-and-roll. She immediately slid into the shadows under the body of the plane.

The Russian jumped down after her. His feet had barely touched the ground before Magnus tackled him and sank his teeth into the man's throat.

Blood splattered the side of the plane as he tore open a carotid artery, but he didn't care. It was a just killing.

The man had taken his Mina. He struggled to not completely lose himself to the wolf's blood lust. During the full moon hunt, he let the wolf celebrate the takedown of prey by feasting on the meat. But this was not venison.

He struggled to control the beast. It protested, so Magnus sent it an image of Mina.

Protect your mate.

The wolf immediately stood down and looked for her.

Mina appeared from underneath the plane and crouched on the ground, one hand stretched out toward them.

"It's okay," she said. "I'm fine. You can shift back now." She looked cautiously toward Arek, who stood to the side, intently focused on Mina. "I'm just going to trust that this is a buddy of yours." She slid closer to Magnus. In his wolf form, he was the size of a small pony. "You're beautiful." She touched the fur on his neck. "You saved me."

A feeling of peace flooded his senses as her fingers brushed his pelt and he changed back to his human form. He buried his nose in her hair. Her scent calmed him further. "Trust me. Just a little."

She sighed. "How can I not?"

Mine, his wolf growled.

Ours, Magnus corrected, and the beast reluctantly agreed.

EPILOGUE

S *ix months later.*

Mina closed her laptop and stretched to work out the kinks in her neck. She'd just emailed her report to another satisfied client. Setting out on her own had been hard at first, but Arek had been an enormous help. He ran a physical security firm—as opposed to Magnus' software security—and Mina's investigative skills had proven themselves a great asset to his business. She helped vet clients and also to track down adversaries that could be the threat that caused some of them to hire Arek in the first place.

She walked out of the spare bedroom that served as her office. The floor-to-ceiling windows facing west showed brilliant blue sky over the snowcapped Rocky Mountains. She'd feel bad about living in this luxurious abode on the top floor of the Four Seasons Private Residences, but her new business earned well, and she liked the secure location. It would be hard for stray wolves, even with the help of dark magic, to reach them here.

Her working with Arek had given Magnus a "consultant to the Pacific Packs" status. He was not a full member, but the ties were close enough to where other alphas had stopped pursuing him.

And she'd come to terms with dating a wolf and working with wolves. Her ex hadn't been a jealous possessive jerk because he was a shifter. He'd been a regular controlling asshole who happened to hide a wolf inside.

"There you are," Magnus said when she reached the living room. He rose from one of the cream-colored couches. His hair stood up on end as if he'd run his fingers through it.

"Is something wrong?"

He took a step toward her but then stopped. Retrieving a small box from his pocket, he kneeled down on one knee. "Mina, marry me." As usual, he made a demand out of what should be a question.

She stared down into the opened box. A big Asscher cut canary diamond surrounded by smaller round-cut white diamonds sparkled in the sunlight. "It's the color of your wolf's eyes."

"That's not an answer."

"There was a question?" She placed the exquisite ring on her finger and stretched her arm out. "It reminds me of a daisy."

"Mina," her fiancé growled.

"Yes," she said and leaned down to kiss her wolf.

A FLASH OF FEAR PREVIEW

*R*ed and blue lights from two police cruisers illuminated the main farmhouse as Molly Nyland drove up the tree-lined driveway. She eased around the medical examiner's transport van and parked next to a gray Ford. The classic sedan-shape of the car, plus the multiple antennas, gave it away as another police vehicle.

She reached for her sketchpad on the passenger seat, opened the door, and slid out of her car. Cradling the pad in the crook of her arm, she paused to smooth down her skirt and snap the cuffs of her sleeves in place. A sigh escaped her lips as she gingerly picked a path through the brown fall grass to the back of the house. Her black leather boots had been stylish in the office of the graphic design firm where she worked full time. They were less practical in the field on her gig as a freelance forensic artist.

"Literally, in the field," she muttered as she avoided a pile of horse manure and walked down the side of the building. Pants and comfortable flats, or even better, rubber boots would not only be more practical but also make her blend in better with the cops. Detective Zedler had been short on the phone, his voice laced with urgency. She hadn't dared take the time to go home and change since the farm was several miles outside of Prairie Falls, and her navigation system was based on the city's official maps. On the rural roads of eastern Washington State, what was planned and what was built didn't always match.

Behind the house, police and crime scene technicians bustled under bright lights powered by generators. Their feet had trampled the dry grass such that it partially covered the cracked mud. Molly scanned the crowd and spotted Zedler at the same time he saw her. The middle-aged detective jogged toward her. His bushy gray eyebrows looked like two caterpillars facing off over kind brown eyes. The tweed jacket he always wore made him look more like a college professor than the seasoned detective he was. Since he'd been somewhat of a mentor to her ever since she moved to Prairie Falls five years ago, the teacher role fit.

"Nyland, about time you got here." He said, slightly out of breath.

Molly fell in step beside him. "What's going on?" On the phone, he'd given her the farm's address and asked her to bring the sketchpad she used when working with kids, but hung up before she had a chance to ask for details.

"We've got a body." He stopped when she froze mid-step and briefly touched her elbow. "You okay?"

Her stomach clenched, but she managed a nod. The medical examiner van should have tipped her off, but she'd worked fifteen cases with Zedler, and none of them involved a death. She rubbed her shoulder where the scars from a lightning strike back when she was twelve were already tingling. The Lichtenberg figure that covered her back, shoulder, and arm in spidery fern-like patterns had been a curse when she was younger, but in college, she'd discovered their advantage. The lightning had given weird scars, but also abilities that made her such an excellent sketch artist.

Sympathy shone in the detective's eyes as he studied her. The eyebrows straightened, the caterpillars relaxing in a temporary truce. "Welcome to your first murder scene, Nyland." He reached out and placed his hand on the small of her back, gently propelling her forward. "Do what you always do. Ask the witness questions and make a brilliant sketch of our suspect. It's not different from what you've done before. Just another crime to solve." As close as she was to the detective, he didn't know about her scars or her ability. She'd only shared that with her best friend.

Molly nodded and took a deep breath to steady herself. "Who's my witness?"

Zedler opened the farmhouse backdoor and chaperoned her across the threshold. "A terrified eight-year-old girl." His voice lowered. "She got up in the middle of the night to get a drink of water and saw a stranger in the back, holding a knife. When he noticed the girl, he rattled the door, but ran away when she screamed."

Molly instantly felt sympathy for the witness. As a little girl, she'd learned to be scared in her own house, but not because of evil outside the walls. In her case, the monsters had been living in the same house as her, calling themselves "family."

As they walked through the kitchen, Molly took in brief impressions of well-worn but gleaming clean counters and wood cabinets. An older white refrigerator hummed in the corner, the low tune of the appliance accompanying the beat of her heels against the linoleum floor. The neat and welcoming home was another contrast to her own upbringing.

Her job tonight came back into focus. A murder.

She'd never drawn a murderer.

Molly swallowed, hard. "Who did he kill?"

"We don't know the victim's identity yet. Neither the girl or her mother has seen him before."

"You showed the girl the body?" Molly's voice rose an octave.

Zedler shot her a look. "Of course not. We showed her a picture of his face. A very peaceful picture without any gore."

They entered a cozy living room where a woman with long brown curly hair sat on a worn beige corduroy sofa, cradling a little girl in her lap as she stroked the child's back. A fire crackled in a large fireplace, its warm glow reflecting off the polished coffee table.

Molly's impractical boots caused her to stumble slightly when the flooring went from linoleum to carpet. Zedler grabbed her elbow and addressed the woman and child on the sofa. "Mrs. Lidgren."

The woman turned, her heart-shaped face pale. The girl peered over her shoulder. She was her mother's carbon copy, reduced in size, except for equally big brown eyes.

"Yes," the mother said, her voice thick.

"This is the forensic artist who will work with Annie."

Molly took a few steps into the room and crouched in front of the little girl. "I like your name, Annie." It earned a small smile. "My name is Molly."

The mother tightened her grip on the child. "Do we really have to do this? She's distraught." Nervous laughter escaped her lips. "As am I. My husband is away this week. To think that a stranger—" Her voice broke.

Molly glanced at the mother before looking into the girl's tear-rimmed eyes. Even with her unique talent, the first few hours after a crime were crucial. After that, witnesses started to forget details. Especially witnesses in shock. "Do you like to draw?"

171

The little girl nodded.

Opening her sketchpad, Molly showed her a drawing of a landscape. "So do I." She flipped the page to show a dolphin jumping over a boat, water splashing the people on the deck.

Annie scooted a little closer, bending over the paper.

The next page showed a court jester tumbling across a pasture filled with horses and cows, the animals laughing at his antics. A tentative smile turned up the corners of the little girl's mouth.

Some of the tension drained out of Mrs. Lidgren's face, and she released her daughter, keeping only an arm around Annie's back. "How about you make a drawing with Molly?" She stroked her daughter's cheek.

"Okay," Annie whispered, scooting off her mother's lap to sit fully on the couch.

Molly sat down beside her and pulled a medium graphite pencil and a kneaded eraser from the hard-plastic case she'd brought in her purse. She flipped to an empty page on the pad. "Why don't you describe who you saw, and I'll try to draw that person."

The little girl nodded.

"Let's start with some easy things. Was it a grown-up?"

Annie nodded again. Her brown eyes focused on Molly.

"Was it a man or a woman?"

The girl whimpered, quickly sliding to her mother and grabbing her hand. Molly envied their closeness. She'd been raised by a grandmother who used spanking as her favorite child-rearing tool. She'd been the last person Molly had turned to for comfort as a child. Extremely religious, home-grown-militia-fan Grammie would do somersaults in her grave if she knew her granddaughter worked for "the bacon," which satisfied Molly in a slightly twisted way.

Mrs. Lidgren caressed Annie's curls. "It's okay, Sweetie. Just tell Molly what you saw."

Annie turned toward Molly, leaning forward a little. "I saw a monster," she whispered.

A small electric current ran down Molly's left shoulder and arm. She made herself sit as still as possible. A kid's imagination could run haywire under stress. The 'monster' description could mean anything, but her Lichtenberg patterns itching conveyed that Annie was on the right track. They just needed to flush out the details. A completely incorrect description would make the scars on Molly's back react. "Okay," she positioned the pencil on the pad, "tell me what the monster looked like. Did he have a small or big head?"

"Big."

Molly continued asking questions about eyes, nose, chin, mouth, and teeth. She pulled out more pencils of various hardness from her case and filled in the drawing in multiple shades of gray and black. After each feature, she swiveled the pad toward Annie and adjusted anything the girl wanted changing. A broad face slowly grew on the page. Wide-set eyes, which Annie described as black, gazed out of the paper straight at Molly. She shivered as the scars on both her back and shoulder went haywire. That was a new sensation, one she didn't know how to interpret.

"More dark," Annie touched the paper and smudged the pupil. "His eyes were black all over."

Molly filled in the whites of the eyes with quick strokes. "Like this? Are you sure?"

The little girl nodded, and they continued building the rest of the man's features. A nose with a long straight ridge and flared nostrils hovered over thick lips stretched into a snarl, showing white cusped teeth.

Zedler sat on the couch across the coffee table and watched the procedure. Molly could feel his eyes focusing on her as she asked each question.

"What did his ears look like?"

Annie paused. Her voice had grown stronger and more confident with each detail added to the drawing, but now it was barely above a whisper again. "Like Batman."

Molly's back tingled and itched. She couldn't help but squirm on the sofa. Out of the corner of her eye, she saw Zedler leaning forward, studying her. His eyes seemed too intense, too focused on her. When he saw her noticing his gaze, he relaxed into the back of the couch.

She turned her attention back on Annie, ignoring the familiar pins and needles still fluttering on her back, down the white web of disfigurement, left shoulder, and arm. She shifted on the couch. As much as she loved what she did as a forensic artist, she hated those scars. They marked her as a freak and were also the reason Grammie had escalated from regular spanking to full-on beatings that she thought would drive the evil out of her only grandchild. The pastor of the fundamentalist church that Grammie and Molly's Great Uncle had attended, insisting that the devil had put his mark on Molly's skin.

The tingling on her back didn't indicate that Annie was lying. The little girl just couldn't find the correct words to match the picture her mind recalled. And somehow the Lichtenberg pattern picked up on the mismatch. She now knew that oddities like hers were appeared often in lightning victims, at least in those who survived. That had been of little comfort when she was a little girl, and Grammie referred to the scars as "the mark of the devil." When the beatings didn't work, she'd tried to starve the evil out of her granddaughter by locking Molly in a closet.

She felt Zedler watching her again. Frowning, she picked up the pencil. Had he picked up on her skin's reaction? She hadn't shared her abilities with him. Being one of the few women working with the police force and the only forensic artist made her an oddity enough.

"Like Batman," she replied cheerfully to Annie. "Do you mean he had pointy ears?"

The girl nodded. "They were sharp, like Batman's, but not on the top of the head, on the side, like mine." She cupped her own ears.

Molly's shoulder stopped itching. She drew human ears, pointed at the top.

Annie peered at the drawing for a few minutes when Molly turned the sketchpad around. The little girl's breath hitched. "Longer."

Molly adjusted the shape of the ears, keeping her eyes on the page while she asked another question. "What about the hair? Short? Long?"

"Like Austin Moon's."

Mrs. Lidgren intervened. "She watches reruns of *Austin & Ally* on the Disney Channel. He has shaggy half-long hair."

Molly didn't know the program but sketched the shaggy just-above-the-ears style that had been preferred by teenaged boys around Prairie Falls a few years ago. She showed Annie.

"More bangs."

Molly complied and twisted the pad around again.

Annie gasped. "That's him." She pointed to the paper, and then quickly pulled her hand back as if the figure would pop out of the page and bite her.

Mrs. Lidgren met Molly's eyes above her daughter's head, her palm stroking Annie's hair. "I don't know how much this will help you." She gestured toward the drawing on Molly's lap. "But thank you for being kind to Annie." She turned to Zedler. "If it's okay, I'll take Annie upstairs."

The detective nodded and addressed the little girl. "You have been so helpful, Annie. Thank you very much for being brave."

Mrs. Lidgren stroked her daughter's cheek. "Sweetie, how

about we go upstairs to see Teddy? He'll probably want a hug just about now."

"Okay." The little girl slid off the couch and walked out of the room. Her little feet beat at staccato as she ran up the stairs.

Her mom followed at a more sedate pace.

Zedler peered down on the page in the sketchpad. "Who is that? Some comic book character?"

Molly shrugged. "The shock of seeing a stranger, the darkness, the shadows, witnessing a violent attack, they all combine to create this picture in her mind." Annie had described exactly what she'd seen, but what had emerged on the sketchpad didn't look remotely human.

Zedler sat down on the coffee table, still staring at the picture. "Nobody looks like this. Do you think he's wearing a mask or something?"

Molly suppressed a shiver as she looked back down at the otherworldly creature whose eyes drank darkness. "Could be. This is who Annie remembers in the backyard."

Zedler sighed. "If you say so. At least we tried." He stood. "Come back outside with me. I want you to meet our new detective, a transfer. His name is Rankin."

Heat rushed through Molly. That name, surely it couldn't be the same man she knew—had known. Her mind flash-backed on calloused palms sliding up her thighs, lighting her skin on fire. She quickly suppressed the memory and slowly put away the pencils and the eraser to hide her shaking hand.

Oblivious to the turmoil going on inside her, Zedler waited impatiently. "You may know of him, he's from California."

Molly had been able to start working with Prairie Falls PD as soon as she'd moved to the city because the lieutenant for whom she'd freelanced while at Santa Clara University, had given his recommendation. For a short time, she'd been on loan to the Sacramento PD and had worked with someone named Rankin—and made a poor decision—but the universe couldn't be that cruel. There must be more than one Detective Rankin from California. Either way, she was in deep shit. Just the mention of his name had her blushing like crazy. She wished it was out of embarrassment, but the truth was that the details of that very unwise, but oh so pleasurable, decision were still vivid in her mind. "But shouldn't I drop the sketch off at the station?" If this was the same Rankin, she would not be able to deal with him right now. Not this close to doing a sketch. Working with a witness always drained her.

Zedler studied her face. "Are you okay? You look a little flushed."

"I'm fine." She fiddled with her sketch pad.

He shrugged. "Drop the sketch off later. I want you to meet Rankin. You two will be working together." He gestured for her to walk out ahead of him.

As she crossed the kitchen this time, her heels against the floor echoed *trou-ble, trou-ble, trou-ble.*

A LIGHT RAIN had started to fall, and Detective Desmond Rankin wished he'd brought more suitable clothes than just his favorite leather jacket. Through the drizzle, he saw the shadowy shapes of Zedler and a woman exit the farmhouse. Good thing they'd set up the tarp tent over the crime scene before the weather turned. The white plastic would protect any ground evidence.

The senior detective and, judging from her oversized drawing pad, the sketch artist, trudged across the field. Zedler's shoulders slumped, and he looked more rumpled than usual. The little girl witness must not have been much help.

As they got closer, Des sucked in a breath. He'd recognize that wavy red hair and the gentle sway of her hips anywhere. His hands clenched at the memory of caressing those curves. He thrust them into the pockets of his jacket to stop them from reaching out. The last time he saw Molly Nyland, she'd been up against a wall with him buried deep inside her.

Correction.

The last time he saw Nyland, she'd scrambled into her jeans before bolting out the door, mumbling something about "a mistake" and "being on the rebound."

Raindrops glistened in Zedler's hair and bushy eyebrows as he approached Des. "Any news?"

Des zipped up his jacket against the night chill and glanced toward the corner of the clearing where the techs were still working under a hastily constructed white tarp tent. The medical examiner had just removed the body. "Nothing good." He flicked a quick glance at Nyland, she refused to meet his eyes.

Great. This wouldn't be awkward at all.

She looked good. A little pale, which made her adorable freckles stand out more starkly. The designer duds she wore —so different from the jeans and long-sleeved t-shirts she'd always worn when they worked together—hugged a lush body in all the right places. The past five years had obviously treated her well.

Back when he'd known her, she was in her last year of college and making some money on the side through forensic sketching. She'd done some work for the Santa Clara PD, and their lieutenant recommended her to Des' department in Sacramento when they couldn't catch a break in a string of violent home invasions and robberies. Nyland's sketch of a potential suspect had been released to the media, and within two days, they'd arrested the perp.

Zedler sighed, interrupting Des' recollection. "That would be too much to hope for." He lightly touched Nyland's elbow. "This is Molly Nyland, our forensic artist. She's the best, we're lucky to have her work with us."

"We've met." Des' words came out harsher than he intended. He cleared his throat. "We worked a case together in Sacramento." He held out his hand. "Good to see you again, Nyland." Silently he congratulated himself on how normal he acted. As if she hadn't been on his mind ever since she bolted out of his apartment. As if he hadn't tried to find her through social media when she left Santa Clara. He'd refused to use the police databases to search for her. That reeked of too much desperation. Even he had a little bit of pride left to salvage. Not much after Mitchell's death, but Des held on hard to the few crumbs that were still there.

She finally had to look at him, but her gaze quickly darted away. At least she shook his hand, but then dropped it like it burned. "Good to see you too."

Des ignored Zedler's puzzled look. Fuck, he didn't even know what had happened between Nyland and himself, never mind trying to explain it to someone else. He'd been in trouble as soon as he'd seen her walk into the Sacramento PD headquarters, those five years ago. The only thing that had kept him from claiming her right away was that sleeping with coworkers was never a good idea, plus everything about her had said "relationship girl." And Des didn't do long-term.

But the night they caught that perp, all his noble intentions had gone to shit. He could blame it on the celebratory tequila shots, but the truth was he could no longer resist the chemistry that sizzled between them. She must have noticed those spark as well because she'd been watching him too. Her gray eyes hesitant, but enticing, daring him to make a move. So he did, and then the joke had been on Des when "relationship girl" hadn't wanted anything to do with him after he'd made her come against the wall of the entrance hall in his apartment. He was slightly ashamed over how eager he had been. He'd reached for her as soon as the door closed behind them. Hadn't even taken the time to get her all the way into the bedroom. Shit, the encounter had been so quick, he didn't even get her shirt off.

And yet, he still couldn't get that brief hook-up out of his mind. However, much had happened since then. He was a very different man, a different cop, now. The death of a partner would do that, and considering she couldn't even look him in the eye this many years after, he should stay well clear of Nyland. He shot her another brief glance before concentrating back on work, a true and tested escape when things got complicated.

"We still haven't been able to ID the victim. No wallet, or anything else in his pockets. We've expanded the search parameter, but so far all we've found is grass and mud, and more mud," he said to Zedler.

"Any tracks?" the older detective asked.

"Tons of them, from animals. Goats apparently graze back here all the time, and this is where the farmer trains his dogs to herd." Des wished he had something to share. As the new transfer on the squad, he needed to prove himself. Clearing a murder—the first PFPD had experienced in more than a decade—would go a long way toward earning respect from his new colleagues. He was hoping it would be enough to have them ignore the ugly gossip that would sooner or later catch up with him from Sacramento. When your partner died under mysterious circumstances, the boys and girls in blue became uncomfortable with you. Des knew that from first-hand experience.

Had Nyland heard the rumors? The thought bothered him more than it should.

He forced his mind away from her. She would be a distraction he couldn't afford. He'd come to Prairie Falls for a fresh start, but also to shake down the vague connection between Mitchell and this place. He hadn't expected to find a department full of hardworking and honest policemen and women, but he did, and he liked them. And he wanted them to like him.

Plus, this particular case had already gotten under his skin. He wanted to nail the sick-shit who'd gone after a scared little kid after killing someone in her back yard. Des was good at catching bad guys, and this one seemed particularly sadistic. The adult male victim had been hung by his feet and drained. They'd found enough splatter to know he'd been alive before hung in the tree at the farm, but most of the blood had been removed. This murderer was one sick fucker. "Was the little girl at least able to provide a description of who she saw?"

Zedler looked at Nyland, but she seemed to find her boots extremely interesting and wouldn't look up. The detective cleared his throat. "The kid did good, but she's only eight. In her mind, she saw a monster, so that's what she described."

Des nodded. Young witnesses were hit or miss, especially when they were scared or shocked. "What next?"

"You know the drill. Keep canvassing the area. Pick up every little thing you find. Bag it, tag it, and send it to the lab for analysis."

"That's all?" Des couldn't help but ask.

The other detective briefly squeezed Des' shoulder. "That, and hope for the autopsy to give us clues. Oh, and it would be good if dental records gave us an ID of the poor guy." He sighed again. "I've got to go talk to the techs." He turned to Nyland. "You'll be okay?"

She nodded.

Zedler gave Des a questioning look before taking off.

Des shrugged in response even though he wasn't sure what the question had been.

He stood quietly next to Nyland as they watched Zedler follow the yellow tape along the cordoned area until he reached the end where the crime scene technicians were picking up nearly microscopic fragments from the ground. Probably none of them useful.

The silence stretched on. As the rain drizzled down, Des considered offering her his jacket, but some perverse passive-aggressive side of him refused the gesture. After hastily climbing off his dick and bolting out the door, she hadn't bothered to return any of his calls or texts.

"So you left Santa Clara," he finally threw out without taking his eyes off Zedler.

In his peripheral vision, he saw her turn to him with a puzzled look on her face. "I got offered a job at a design firm here in Prairie Falls right after graduation."

If her forensic sketches were any indication of her design skills, she'd probably had loads of job offers. "And how do you like it?"

"The job or the town?" She shivered in the rain.

He faced her. "Both, I guess."

Strands of hair lay plastered against her cheeks. Des's hands unclenched in his pockets as he wanted to wipe the rain from her face. He shoved them deeper into his jacket and then cursed under his breath and pulled them out. Des unzipped his coat and shrugged out of it before sweeping it around her shoulders, refusing to dwell on how her wearing his jacket satisfied something deep inside him.

She pulled the coat tighter. "The job is competitive but

interesting, and I've learned tons. I work with cutting edge design methods and software, and the firm uses innovative marketing strategies. It was a good place to start, and now a great place to work."

"And the town?" he prodded.

She cocked her head. "You're here now. What do you think?"

He had almost forgotten how she could go from shy to sassy in seconds. He bowed his head to hide the smile playing in the corner of his mouth. "I've only been here a few weeks. Other than fast-food joints and the police station, I haven't seen much of it."

She grinned. "Still maintaining a healthy diet of grease and milkshakes?"

"You know me, body by burgers." He patted his thankfully-still-flat stomach. Now that he'd passed thirty, he actually had to pay attention to what he ate. And spend more time in the gym. But there was no way he'd let Nyland know that little metabolic fact.

She chuckled weakly. "It's a nice town. With three hundred thousand people, it's large enough to have some culture—we have a vibrant theatre community and a symphony—but still small enough to almost have everyone being connected to everyone else, somehow."

Des knew the size of the population but hadn't bothered learning about the cultural amenities. He'd just been happy to transfer out of Sacramento after Mitchell's murder. The town that his partner had jotted down in a notebook having positions open was a happy coincidence. Besides, as long as there was a movie place, he had all the culture he needed. "You don't miss California? The weather?" Eastern Washington winters could be brutal, he'd heard.

A shadow chased across Nyland's face, and she quickly glanced down. "No, I'm good with having four seasons again." She looked up at him, her features neutral again. "Plus, my best friend from college lives here."

He wanted to ask more about where she grew up and who her best friend was, but he didn't know where to start. They'd never discussed anything but work. And never really been alone together except for that one night when she came home with him.

And stayed only long enough to get her rocks off.

Nyland interrupted his thoughts. "I should get back into town and drop the sketch off at the station." She pulled off his jacket while balancing her sketchpad in one hand. "Thanks for lending me this."

"Keep it. I can get it from you later."

She shook her head, holding out his coat. "Thanks, but I'll be okay until I get to the heater in the car."

He pulled on his jacket and zipped up the front as he watched her leave. The hem of her skirt swung back and forth, flirting with the top of her tall boots, utterly inappropriate for a farm and mud.

The cold rain came down harder. Maybe Des should follow and make sure she got to the car safely. He flipped up his jacket collar to stop icy drops from snaking their way inside his shirt and down his back. The jacket smelled like a combination of vanilla and citrus, a fragrance that was uniquely hers. He took a step after Nyland.

"Rankin, get back here," Zedler shouted from behind. "We may have something."

Des sighed and jogged across the field.

"What did you find?" he asked as he reached Zedler, who held a plastic evidence bag up to the light.

"Check this out." The older detective showed the bag toward Des. "What do you make of this?"

A strip of metal glittered in the high-powered crime scene lights. "Is that gold?" Des turned the item over in his hand. "It looks like a hand-held sickle." Twelve inches long and about half an inch wide, the grip of the curved blade would fit comfortably in his palm.

Zedler nodded and traced a finger on top of the curved blade through the transparent plastic. "Gold or some alloy of it. What about these symbols?"

The gold—if it was gold—was stamped with Russian letters or something belonging on a fraternity sign. "Cyrillic or Greek?"

"Don't know," Zedler said. "The techs say it's a possible match to the wounds on the victim's neck."

"Shit. Is this some kind of weird ritual killing? Drain the body of blood using a weirdo knife?"

Zedler shrugged. "Your guess is as good as mine. We'll get an expert on it, but let's go see if this is the weapon Annie saw in the monster's hand." He walked toward the house.

Des trailed after, still studying the weird blade and letters. Something nagged at him in the back of his mind, but whatever it was slid just beyond his focus. It would come to him eventually.

* * *

To READ Des and Molly's story, order Flash of Fear today!

Join my VIP Readers List to gain access to exclusive content and giveaways:
www.asamariabradley.com/newsletter/

ACKNOWLEDGMENTS

There's always a team behind every novel and for this one, I leaned on a lot of fabulous and generous people.

A very special thank you to Liz Berry, Jillian Stein, and MJ Rose. Without the 1,001 Dark Nights short story challenge, there would be no *Norse Billionaire Shifters* series!

Keyanna Butler of Elle Woods PR did an amazing job getting the word out about this book. She was also there for support and encouragement when I had neurotic writer moments. Also thank you to all the bloggers, reviewers, and influencers who gave this book shout-outs.

For fun chats, support, rant-listening, and needed kicks in the butt, I owe thanks to authors Piper J. Drake, Katee Robert, and to my Arctic Thunder sisters: Rebecca Zanetti and Boone Brux.

Also a HUGE thank you to my friends and family, your support of and faith in me means the world. Special shout-out to my bestie Jere', who's always there, whether I need to celebrate or rant.

My life would be very bleak if I didn't have my husband

by my side. He is my biggest supporter, and my most constructive critic, depending on what I need most in that moment.

And finally, the biggest THANK YOU goes to the readers. Without you, there would be no books! <3

ABOUT ASA MARIA BRADLEY

Asa Maria Bradley grew up in Sweden surrounded by archaeology and history steeped in Norse mythology, which inspired her sexy modern-day *Viking Warriors* and *Norse Billionaire Shifters* paranormal romance series. She also writes urban fantasy about empowered heroines who kick ass while saving the world.

Booklist attributes her writing with "nonstop action, satisfying romantic encounters, and intriguing world building" and *Entertainment Weekly* says "when it comes to paranormal romance with explosive action scenes, Bradley has that nailed." Her work has received the honors of a double nomination for the Romance Writers of America's RITA contest, a Reviewers' Choice Award nomination, a Holt Medallion win, and a Booksellers' Best Award win.

Asa came to the United States as a high school exchange student and quickly fell in love with ranch dressing and crime TV dramas of all flavors, two addictions she unfortunately still struggles with. Currently, she lives on a lake deep in the forest of the Pacific Northwest with a British husband and a rescue dog of indeterminate breed. Sadly, neither of them obeys any of her commands.

Connect with Asa on her website: www. AsaMariaBradley.com. To stay up to date on new releases, receive exclusive content, have access to fabulous giveaways, and receive access to Asa's free reads, sign up for her VIP Reader List at: www.asamariabradley.com/newsletter.

- facebook.com/AsaMariaBradley.Author
- twitter.com/AsaMariaBradley
- instagram.com/asamariabradley
- amazon.com/author/asamariabradley
- bookbub.com/authors/asa-maria-bradley
- goodreads.com/asamariabradley

ALSO BY ASA MARIA BRADLEY

For the most current list, please visit
www.AsaMariaBradley.com/books.

The *Norse Billionaire Shifters* Series

(Paranormal Romance)

A Wolf's Hunger

A Wolf's Obsession

A Wolf's Craving

The *Powers of Lightning* Series

(Urban Fantasy/Supernatural Suspense)

Flash of Fear

Flash of Fate

The *Viking Warriors* Series

(Paranormal Romance)

Viking Warrior Rising

Viking Warrior Rebel

Loki Ascending

The Theia Ayer Series

(Urban Fantasy)

Siren's Storm

The Sea King's Daughters: Collection 2

A Grifter's Song **Multi-Author Series**

(Crime Fiction)

Upgrade

A Grifter's Song Vol. 3

Printed in Great Britain
by Amazon

72022867R00118